STARLINGS

STARLINGS

Miranda Gold

KARNAC

First published in 2016 by
Karnac Books Ltd
118 Finchley Road
London NW3 5HT

British Library Cataloguing in Publication Data

A C.I.P. for this book is available from the British Library

ISBN-13: 978-1-78220-509-8

Typeset by Medlar Publishing Solutions Pvt Ltd, India

Printed in Great Britain

www.karnacbooks.com

For Matt

PART ONE

L ess than an hour ago I was taking the same step past my mother's door, stepping back, raising my hand to knock, dropping it—she's a light sleeper, my mother, very light: I wouldn't want to wake her, not if she's managed to drop off, at least for a bit—but there it was, her dream-coated slur calling out:

Be with me, be with me, why will you never be with me?

Her voice but a ghost's words, the last shards of a dream she's always had. I can leave but her dream comes with me—she comes with me. Even now, two bus rides away from the house, I can still hear her—her note, her beat—the beat of the infant-mother, pulsing under the babble at Victoria station.

London to Brighton. Eight minutes. Platform six.

After the rushing and the shoving, that beat is all that's left: an empty iron fortitude, refusing to be beaten down by the clamour. How can such a little cry have such strength? Ensuring I remember, just as it pretends to help me forget:

Be with me, be with me, why will you never be with me?

But then the infant's note in my mother's voice hollows to an empty shell, drily scoring the passage from city to sea.

"Is that your father?" she'd asked, just as I was about to make my way. "Is it? Ask him to come up to me. He said he'd—"

"He's coming," I'd said, half looking, not looking at him at the bottom of the stairs, the obligatory chipped white saucer in his hands, eyes closing inside the outline of a face blunted by familiarity telling me I'd missed the long breath and the ash sigh that aren't meant for hearing. He'd looked up, open eyes walking the flight he always seemed to be preparing himself for, the quick, slight tuck of his chin inviting me to go down first, nodding at my bag, at me, mouth indicating a smile.

"Clunk click and all that," he said.

"I'm taking the train," I said.

"Of course you are." The smile had wandered into his eyes for a moment and I waited for that Hello of his he always gives me to deliver to my brother Steven every time I go Brighton to visit—say hello to the boy for me won't you, he always says—but he didn't, just took the steps his eyes had climbed, opening the bedroom door as I closed the front door behind me, just catching the last of the infant-mother beating her old refrain—

Be with me, be with me, why will you never—?

Her note, that beat, merging with the hum under the city but, soon as Steven meets me off the train, he'll haul it onto his back along with my bag, carry its weight, its pitch, it will start to fade then—it always does, finds no milk in the dry breast of indifference—it's the way he barely seems to feel its strain, effortless, doesn't tug against him, makes it all go quiet somehow.

Steven left way back but really it's fine because it's not like Brighton's far, you can do it in a day, easy—"'You could just come for the day, you know Sal." That's what he said last time. He's right of course, I could, I know I could, but it's always been three days, we need three days—I need three days—it's always been … Truth is we can play out the pattern in an evening, less, but it wouldn't be the same, dashing off just as we're easing in—as I'm easing in. The pattern. I like the regularity of it: get back to the guest house where Steven lives and works now, endure gin rummy, or, with a bit of luck, sometimes just gin, with Clive, the landlord, drop my bag but take a scarf out in case the wind picks up, go off for our fish supper, a stroll, a paddle. Yes, that's how it goes, how it's meant to go—at least that's how it went the first year—four years ago that was now—didn't quite manage to play out the pattern in full last time, or the time before, but this year … yes, I suppose I could just be going for the day.

Boarding the train is enough to flatten the note of the infant, but I can feel the beat of the mother, gathering up to a slow steady drum as the train staggers on to its course, juddering through the tunnel, finding its rhythm. In the light of the carriage the window opposite sends my face back to me, freezing then flickering; travellers tighten beside me: contracting they grow rigid, warding off the awkward proximity of other bodies—the brushed shoulder, the knocked knee, their resolute inertia now caught, now mocked, splintered and broken by the faithless mirror of the window, promiscuously glancing from train to track. On into the half-light, the adolescent silence of a sour milk March sky softens and gives way to lilac grey dusk, and the wafer-thin copies of jostling faces and papers strobe onto a screen shared with the city's blind rush home. The darkening tower blocks disperse, clinging to the last threads of light failing them fast and, frail without the city's sleepless glare to hold them, urban ghosts glide by and vanish. The view, almost a blind, hints only the outlines of a trackside house: filtering through faceless it slips under my face, grabs my blurred features before stealing the face yawning beside me, a moment snatched then discarded.

The window's eye inverts, gets lost in a navel-gaze, roving drunken to conjure a twin for each unhidden head, doubled up by its giddy laugh—the puerile chuckle of the funfair mirror seems to prod the sleepers awake, enrage a careless hand as it leafs through a book, the daily commute becomes a slow-motion circus.

The beat feeds off my jittery reflection, won't be soothed by the train's motion—a wiry pulse throbbing at my soles. A gentle snore beside me. Moment of vicarious respite, marvel at his oblivion. He doesn't feel the beat, doesn't hear it, no, heard nothing, felt nothing, this suit who'd boarded two stops ago and, having whisked out report and pen, promptly let his head loll back and fall to a shoulder, the report waving out of an unconscious hand. My eyes dart up to his fretful double and from here inspect the ensemble: only a boy shooting his rocket as high as his arm would reach and crash landing it into his father's insensible cheek seems to play with the image of his fantastic proportions—the eye requires no consent to play, mindless alchemy, it fashions a pantomime from interchangeable puppets. The train jolts to a stop, the suit wakes, snatches up his report and catches my eye in the eye of the window, the two eyes snigger—voyeur; carriage etiquette has been breached. The sight of his reflection winds the pulse faster, sharper.

Seven twenty-two. Twelve minutes to stall a crescendo: scrutinise fingernails, skirt pleat, shoelaces—medicate with the mundane till the train lurches to its final stop. See how the babe sups on her sweet dummy, empty feed to still the infant-mother, bolster resistance with banality—not long now till Steven meets me off the platform, most the infant-mother can do then is try to reach a wasted tentacle back towards me, groping weakly for her feed. Apparent indifference might be the finest of Steven's arts but I can't think of it like that; all my faith is built on the lie of careless oblivion he makes seem true—have to believe he's as oblivious as the suit on the train—sure that suit's still sniggering—as the head I see now, flitting into the corner of my eye, competing with attention to thumbnail, jutting chicken-like in frenzied time with a less than personal stereo, same song on repeat since Clapham. Marvellous. Mute to all three—the beat doesn't slacken though, not until it's taken under the clunking boots of Steven's easy strides from station to guest house, managing little more than a gasp in the gaps of our chatter, the cracks in the pavement until, crushed underfoot, it tries to recover the sinews of its shredded musculature between nicety and monosyllable. Another of Steven's arts, equally fine, admirable economy dispensed with inflections, never tolerated waste, very frugal, though he does of course allow for a half-swallowed "not bad", if I remember correctly—I should run through the formula that takes us from platform to guest house, always have to race to keep up with Steven's stride—be alright, won't we? ... The dull but necessary certainty offered by details can be measured by their irrelevance: bypassing skirt pleat, my eyes exchange thumbnail for shoelace. Double bow to be safe, still no guarantee, always coming undone, always at the risk of toppling, even without the beat so hard at my soles. Best pull them a little tighter—the beat is only ever still so long, won't be hushed till it's caught up by the waves gently rocking the pulse to sleep and lulled, fall beneath the opal tide, sinking to its soft crib in the bed of the sea, safely nestled as the waves sing to her and over her, inaudible, innocuous.

Three days the beat seems to sleep—the three day reprieve—least so long as we have our feet in water, go for our little paddle in the shallows, the ritual paddle before the ritual feast—I'd make the pilgrimage for the paddle alone. Remember how it slept that first year I came to visit—never so much as ventured up on shore, it was only later, the infant-mother started wrestling in her nest, threatening hunger unchoked by the fronds, baby fists beating against tight seaweed swaddling, writhing in her binds, the pulse of necessity breaking her free. I've always known there's something ravenous in it, something beyond the infant, beyond the mother, severing them to reach for untold stories and silenced voices, a craving and raging that one day will scavenge the debris, feeding on faeces and entrails to nourish back a lost pitch, and swollen rise, an ancestral curse pounding a torment three generations unspent, the sea's varnished ripples whipped to rabid crests: infant-mother bleating by the bedside seems only to cry *be with me, be with me* but this heart-wrung heartbeat beats till it bursts deadbeat—dead-beat, death-march—a feeble cry in pale pink nightie shrouds the surging roar of the sea-monster's army, latent in depths as we paddle the shallows, the righteous strike of a robbed trident waiting to whirl a moon-glittered course to an opal storm.

We will shortly be arriving in Brighton where this train will terminate.

I stare through him before I see him. It's getting harder each year to register his face: gaunt and stubbled, hiding the candyfloss-cheeked cherub—the little sticky angel-brother Steven I first walked the pier with: hands glued, clasp peeled apart as we each took a leg up for a ride on a painted horse, round and round—"Again, again!"—round till we were sick. Harder and harder each year. Can't seem to find him in that face. But I—I still tie double bows.

I squint my eyes in the drizzle, fathom the brother preserved by memory—the image of that sparkling imp warmed and embellished in rebellious inverse proportion to the ebb of its reality—from the spare dim face and figure coming towards me flash cards unreel in an immediate regression that restore him back to his original template, so that at the last of his stiffened steps to me bright imp is grafted back onto the vacant stranger now

8

stooping at once to just brush coarse lips against my cheek and take my bag—that dual purpose stoop again—chivalry revised with economy, sentiment refined with efficiency: the multitasking knight of the new millennium—the beat tightening at his absent kiss, slackening at his nimble grasp. He straightens and pauses just long enough to abridge my name before he turns so that there's no time to question at which point "Sally" had been deemed excessive—when did I become "Sal" when I had always been "Sally"?

"Sal": wisp of a name sent over my shoulder, drifting into the drizzle, dribbling onto the track. The beat begins its tick. Already he's weaving a passage out of the station—sifting, ploughing: through the milling couples 'mid dawdling reunion, token baffled tourists blinded by redundant map carving county to multicoloured maze, mothers crouching, sandwiched between toddler and suitcase, smartly scrubbing a spittle-dabbed fingertip against a toffee smeared cheek, clock-watching welcome parties, and timetable gazers—the obstacle course stalling the commuters, the pleasure seekers home and bingo bound, Steven as agile in his exit away from me as he was awkward towards me. I follow the top of his head over the crowd, grope a crab-like path to catch up, last steps a clumsy breathless skip, wince as the beat skids—the wrench and retch of the roller coaster without the glee. But there he is, easily hitching my bag up a touch on his back and on his way again. No, didn't feel a thing. Unwitting chivalry. Automated. Took it without a thought. Not a thing, never seemed to feel a thing.

* * *

Couldn't help but wonder at it—how he could just—no matter what—always manage to seem glazed and cool as china—but surely he must have felt it?—Truth was he did—well of course he did and really that was the worst part—seeing the beat catch

hold in him too—could hardly stand to look at him that time—
must be five, six years ago—when I saw the blank mask he'd
set slip, and then, falling away with it, the possibility that there
might still be a sparkling imp hiding beneath—no, the imp had
long gone and taken my little sticky angel brother with it—no,
no imp, but a face beneath nakedly holding a mirror to my own,
the same dart and grasp in it, the twitching of questions waiting,
of silence clenched white with kept answers—how and why and
when—his face, my face, drawing itself in tighter and tighter as
that same inconsolable cry beat through him as it beats through
me—and wanting to say something, because I could see—

"Steven—"

"What?"—The face and voice cracked together—

"Steven—"

"Don't—"

So I didn't, just waited while he reset the mask back over the
face that had betrayed him, aligning the nudged emptiness
of an unlettered counter on the Scrabble board—but still the
beat of the infant-mother, her raw heart throbbing—beating
through him, through me, through us all—all gnawed raw till
it burst—

Dead beat—

Beat away at him till he couldn't feel a—

The mask had set then, moulding the face beneath to its
likeness—never saw Steven's face again in that house and if
the imp and a certain little sticky angel boy had long gone,
whatever of Steven that had remained left then too—maybe
he'd already left—liked to think I'd found him since—that first
year—that was him … might have been—

* * *

Just outside the station a baritone Scot calls after Steven but the name takes a moment too long to catch up with him because the baritone didn't say Steven, he said Mr Brody. Maybe it sounded strange to Steven too—Steven wasn't Mr Brody—Dad is Mr Brody and Steven is—well, he's Steven. The baritone takes off his bowler hat and draws an arc with it to his chest, thick lips tucking themselves in for a camel smile.

"Nine o'clock then, Mr Brody," the baritone says.

I ask Steven who that was, taking two steps for each of his and, of course, Steven just says, "What? Who? Oh, no one."

* * *

Steven. Armoured by apathy, by distance, by time too—three years, no, must be more by now, almost four, four this Easter, Easter Sunday after the eggs then biked his way to Brighton. We hadn't done Easter before and weren't about to start—and to think now—almost comical—all because we'd missed Passover. It didn't seem it would be much odds, it wasn't as if we really did the holidays anymore, hadn't really thought about it until I came back home that evening to see the candles almost out and the Haggadah open at the four sons—I should have been in, stupid really, shouldn't have agreed to do that last minute viewing at the gallery, wouldn't have been so hard to get someone else to spout that script we all had by rote just for the sake of this grotesque rendering of a broken-backed donkey. I tried to joke Dad out of his silence as he came in to pour away Elijah's cup, face unsettled in the tremor of the light, saying we could always make up for it and do Easter instead.

"Well," Dad had said, chewing the bitter herb, "Jesus always was a nice Jewish boy."

Roses are reddish

Violets are bluish

If it wasn't for Christ we'd all be—

So we did Easter: Steven and I had sat there, picking and nibbling at the chocolate shells, kitchen door ajar, nightie-clad mother hovering just behind, Dad smoothing and folding the shiny wrapping so carefully unpeeled—"It is always so satisfying", he'd told us solemnly, "when you can make it so that none of the edges overlap"—and ran a confident nail down each side of his gold foil diamond.

The door opening a crack more:

"Talking about me again, I can hear you talking about me—"

"No one's talking about you," Dad had said, saying what he always said, maybe what he had to say, his eyes closing, Steven's eyes already rolling hard at the ceiling—

"Yes you were—all of you—talking about me—"

"No one was—why don't you come in, sit down with us?"

"What are you telling them about me?"

"Nothing—now why don't—"

"One day I'll go, one day I'll be gone—" she had stopped then, tugging at the sleeve of her nightie where the seam had come loose, twisting a little of its pale comfort round her fingers, her face morphing from mother to infant and back, pulsing in the struggle to coalesce—"You know what they'll say then, don't you? You know what they'll say about you …"

So we nibbled and picked, picked and nibbled; Dad squared and smoothed, sighed, drifted out and upstairs; the threat limped its way back to bedside, faltered, fell, the sighs dragging after, resigned to follow. Steven drew his un-nibbled pickings into a tidy mound, cleared them with his knife into a ready cupped palm, binned them, zipped up the coat he'd worn through the lamb, through the eggs, got up, left. Of course there I was, jolting after him—he'd never tried the cake. He didn't fancy cake. But it was simmel or seminal or something, traditional, for Easter—

"Come on Sal—Easter?"

"I know," I said, a flimsy laugh just breaking through, "Silly—"

Steven shook his head, "No—look it's a nice thought, really, but I'm going to Brighton—I'm not sure I've really got time for cake."

"Oh," I said, "Brighton," the words grim, empty, bouncing off the gnome grinning against the ivy, rebounding and repeating their vacancy, sliding backwards and forwards to see if they might improve their weight, their sense, but they just rolled side to side, two marbles skimming and skating in the bottom of an empty box. Steven tossed the handlebars between hands, my hapless pair of words tossed in time, sliding off the curb as he eased the front wheel onto the road, trailing behind him lethargic, lagging as he shifted gear and rolling into the gutter soon as he sped the corner—away from the beat, the avenue, the city.

Could always make it look like he never felt a thing.

"Went for a nip round the heath, did he?" Dad, off duty, pondering over the kettle, "I used to like that, a nip round the heath on a Sunday."

* * *

"Sorry," I say and the stiff face in front of me now cracks a little, lets me peer through to my brother, glimpse him in a half smile, that closed mouth smile, that half laugh—that's something.

13

"Don't be daft," he says—that's something too—a start, enough to let me feel the relief of unpricked soles—shouldn't fall complacent though, not while we're still a good walk from the waves—I'll need to start reeling it off, something to keep us going—to keep me going—and it's alright, only then I go and tell him how I'd bumped into Melanie of all people the other week—

"Just coming out the Tube," I say. "London Bridge, which was funny because I never usually—Melanie, you can't have forgotten—Aunt Vivien's daughter—" he must remember— "Claire was the older one, then Melanie—the one everyone said looked like—" he'd pulled her hair enough times—"No?"

Steven breathes out just hard enough to break me off. Well, it had been a long time, didn't really keep up with that side of the family—or any side of the family—not now, people always asking questions you didn't have answers for, or not the right answers for—or else the right ones came out wrong— but I'd spent every Tuesday afternoon there right up until our grandfather had died—Melanie and Claire's grandfather too of course but somehow I never thought of him like that—lying on our bellies in the backroom before piano, sharing out crisps and stickers, knowing Mrs Green would be able to tell I hadn't practised and Melanie walking down with me, not a bit scared through the alley into Hodford Road, tummy dipping while the crutches snapped along the floorboards and the red door opened—still, it was better than going home—

"You didn't say anything to Aunt Vivienne now did you?"

Enough fire in my mother's cheeks then not to see the throb of changing faces from infant to mother and back, still up out of bed most days too, would make sure I got myself and Steven something to eat—

"Don't say—you didn't say—"

14

I can't look at Steven for a moment, can only listen to the waves—I blunder on though, find a "just so wonderful be back here now"—a torrent of wonderfuls follow … "wonderful to see you again, wonderful—and looking so well—no really you do …"

I pause, waiting, clinging …

"Not bad," he says.

There it is: *not bad*. I can stop, wait a moment, see if he isn't ready for his turn, stroll a pace or two before I ask about Clive, the guest house, the regulars, the quiz night, yes, safe to stroll a bit—we're close enough to the sea now—can hear the tide breathing out under the last clattering rides at the pier, the jangling promise of the lucky dip, the fistfuls of coppers swallowed and tumbled.

"Clive's kept five free for you," Steven offers, didn't even have to cue him in, so much better that way, rushed into rambling last time after I'd passed on Dad's hello—just the thought of last year enough to stir the beat—stomach quick to clutch—knew then I should have kept that hello for later—and then making it worse by trying to make it better till Steven's quickened step and the constriction in his voice pinched me, choking the hello I'd passed on too soon—wince as I see it all over again—Steven yanking the straps of my bag over his shoulders, lurching ahead then veering round, marble eyes past me, quietly mechanical voice through ventriloquist lips: "What", I remember him asking, "should make you think I would know how Clive is? It's not my business, or yours for that matter—" lips tight as he whipped round and veered off again—"Anyway, Clive's doing my head in," he said, "the place is doing his head in, the whole bloody thing is—"

I'd jumped in then, wanting to sound all light and bright, "I'm not surprised really," I'd said, hearing myself just that bit too loud, unable to make up the half step between us—"Clive's what Dad would call a character—all very well when I've only got to put up with a few days of it, but you've been stuck there for—" halted right there—

"Stuck? I'm not stuck!—as if you're one to talk—anyway if you hate it so much—"

"I don't hate it, I was just saying—"

"Well don't—"

Felt like we were five and eight again only we wouldn't be giggling half an hour later—giggled till we were dizzy with it and couldn't say when Dad asked what was so funny—

Oh, the three day reprieve—if that beating could just stop for three days I could go back to London, back to that house with skin tight enough around me—keep me from falling …

Falling formless, bloodless into the blackness—

"Room five," I say. "Great. Thanks."

Room five, directly above what had become Steven's, metamorphosed in one of Clive's flashes of sheer ingenuity from storage room to room 1b, standard single retaining all original features including dust, several refuse sacks, and, perhaps most crucially of all, the first "room" with the virtues of being both affordable and available four Easter Sundays ago when Steven pitched up with, as Clive would often feel compelled to remind him, "only an empty belly, the clothes on his back, and an ache in his heart", and underwent a second transformation on account of Steven having found his pockets empty within six days, drawing Clive—always eager to expand his kin or workforce—to the inescapably fortuitous conclusion that Steven must be put behind the bar and proudly rechristened room 1b as staff quarters. Room five, it was always room five, always presented as a novelty. Deluxe double, Clive called it, deluxe double as opposed to double

16

deluxe, being, as he was, more sensitive to emphasis than the broken springs of a single mattress. "Bankrupting myself with this generosity of mine," he liked to say, "can't help it, habit of a lifetime"—incurable magnanimity crowned with five per cent knocked off the tariff—"oh and go on, how about a lemon sherbet, seeing as you're part of the family"—"the family" having come to include not only his cherished staff members but, by proxy, their relatives, his regulars (regardless of regularity), and extending (when the philanthropist within him could no longer be restrained) to the boy at the fish counter, the postman, whoever happened to be passing ... "Truly a blessing," he'd proclaim, "to be surrounded by such loyal kin."

Steven tells me Clive insisted on reserving it weeks back.

"Thanks, thank you," I say. "Really good of him—of you—"

"Oh no," Steven says, "Clive, not me. He insisted."

Clive, not him—ready hook for the beat, it latches on, holds tight, winding its way up—dull tick to a quick tap—sticks twitching staccato on a drum skin pulled tight—spurred on as we near the arcade, rising to meet the rush and frenzy of levers wrenched by insatiable hands—come on, laugh, say something, anything, please don't let it be like last time—but it feels just like last time: the beat flares and throbs itself into song, pitched high above the arcade, the clamour spilling from an opened pub door, neglected by the waves, the infant-mother rings right through me—

Be with me—

The infant-mother tugs with her old refrain—could he not hear it, not feel it—that bleating still beating, still bleeding raw: a pitiful hybrid made monstrous, cracked from the shell of a woman our mother had become—

Be with me, why will you never be with—

17

The infant-mother clutches as Steven strides on, the beat harder, her note sharper, a tentacle wraps tight round each ankle, caught up with the infant, caught out by the mother, trips with a comic tumble and back in the circus again: lone player this round, chained bear in the ring unchained cracks a sharp landing of painful shame—Steven three, four, five doorways ahead—he stops, steps back, "Alright Sal," he says, gentleness out of nowhere and maybe he can see another of my sorry's coming because he's mumbling something about Clive through half smiles and half laughs so that all the infant can do is try a last gasping tug, drop and the tentacles uncoil. Spent by her tantrum, the infant-mother lets the next wave curl over her, wrapping her in its deep fold, the Moses basket pulled up from the rushes, carrying with it the phantom pressure pinching in serpentine confession drunk down by the wave and into the liquid black jewel of the sea.

It takes us a few steps but, so long as I keep a decent pace and Steven pulls back, we even ourselves out. Steven's groan about Clive is familiar enough to be a comfort, and, just when I'm not expecting it, there's that mock grunt of his giving way to an irrepressible corner of his mouth—turns up despite all efforts to the contrary, eyes flashing with such a crackle of a chuckle it's almost audible—I think that's him, yes—or close enough— yes, that's my little sticky angel brother.

The guest house is above the pub—all part of the same empire—Clive's empire—and Clive's sitting on a stool at the counter, back turned to the empty tables, conducting the sonata prickling on the record player with a plastic stirrer, so immersed in the rapturous solo of his first violin that it takes more than the creaking open and close of the door to disturb him. Steven stills me a moment with a finger held to his lips and then—last glimpse of the bright imp lost and found—creeps up behind Clive, darts a quick grin back to me and slaps Clive on the back, "Evening, old chap!" he beams at the maestro. Clive jolts, tells Steven what a dreadful little bugger he is, what a cheeky sod, swings round and then, seeing me, curbs his retaliation and swerves into a defiantly serene register: "My dear, good evening," he says, tucking his irritation away under the sheen he works through his voice, an earnest smile smoothed over his lips—a smile that always makes me clutch a skirt pleat in hideous awkwardness—knowing by now this particular smile of Clive's serves as the prologue to the house-special twist of sycophancy and authority that I'm required to indulge for the length of my stay—"Call it service charge"—that's what Steven had said in the end the last time, voice too flat to snap with an old joke that said it was alright—it mightn't have left us dizzy with giggles but then we weren't five and eight and it had been less than half an hour—

Clive starts towards me, halts, edges back, composes himself before erupting with, "My dear! Delightful! Delighted! Charmed!" bouncing each exclamation up several elated octaves above and beyond his abandoned sonata, the last of these plummeting with all the inevitability of gravity and extended for as long as his mighty exhalation would allow so as to ensure his meaning was fully comprehended and— just in case it wasn't—since "one can never be quite sure one is absolutely appreciated"—repeated. "My dear," he says, a flourish of his stirrer aiding his reclamation of propriety, "I was just ..." Another flourish—he frowns at the stirrer, tuts. Steven can't help himself, holds backs the half-smile, suggesting the old maestro is bringing the court to a state of ecstasy. Clive dashes to remove the needle from the record, "So very busy these— run off my—attending to some essential—some crucial—"; interrupted by the discomforting sound of himself breathless and stuttering, Clive pauses, again recomposes and finds a paternal note to test on me, "And how are you my dear?"

"Me?" I look at Steven who comes to my aid with that useless shrug of his. "Fine, I'm fine thanks." I ease the grip of my skirt—I'm fine, fine—and smile at my own caught breath, this is just Clive's way, I'm fine—and then—how does it go? First it's gin rummy with Clive, then Steven and I escape for our fish supper, go for our stroll, our paddle, the ritual paddle ... something like that, that's how it goes, how I thought it all ... was meant to go ... Clive swivels round, dashes back to the bar, rubs his hands together, ducks, and springs back up ("Delighted!") with the serendipitous discovery of—"Rich tea! Now there's a thought! Come on, come on now my dear, don't be shy," and he peers over me as I take one, nodding away until he's satisfied I've made sufficient progress through his offering, "Yes, you see, you see ..." What I'm quite supposed to see I'm not entirely sure but I nod back regardless and smile and this seems to be the correct response as Clive pours us each a gin, pulls out a chair for me, gestures towards one for Steven, sits down, unpockets his cards, and begins shuffling. Steven sighs, relents, takes his place.

"I don't fancy your chances," he says. "I'm on a roll these days," and, after chewing his tongue a moment and taking a considered sip of gin, goes on as he deals, "Ah yes, if you insist ... warned though you are ... treasure in store though for you my dear," he tells me, "treasure indeed." I've barely completed an "Oh yes?" before he's rippling at the thought of showing me, "Room five transformed! A thorough going over has taken place in your absence. A thorough refurbishment. Spring clean, spring polish, slick of new paint no less ... and practically have the place to yourself—queen of the mansion, all quiet on the front, sleep quite sound I'm sure ... Ladies first."

"Place to myself?" I ask, taking a card.

"A quiet moment," Clive looks at Steven, "a *rare* quiet moment—are you going to take that card or are you going to keep us here all bloody night? Quiet my arse thanks to you—I've had that shocker barging in again."

"Always said we should get you a bouncer," Steven says, letting me mistake the bright imp's return. I hadn't heard the arch of a cat's back in his voice—not until the smile I'm too quick to look up with goes unseen, unshared.

"I'll bounce you," Clive tells Steven. "Twice she's been after you now and I'm telling you if that woman—if you could call *her* that—"

"Clive," Steven asks, "you don't mean to tell me you've taken a fancy to Mrs Sergeant?"

"Sergeant Corporal Major for all I care! Not that it's any business of mine what *she* keeps under *her* skirts—peroxide wig, flaming lashes, orange mouth ..."

I try to catch Steven's eye, share the half smile, but there's only the end of a sigh—*leave it Sal, joke's over*, the sigh said.

"This woman,"—no joke to Clive and he's not done with Steven yet—"so-called, wanted to know where that boy of mine was—mine? Well I tell you what, I won't have any of this argy bargy barging in, with a bone to pick"—a bone Clive is quite sure that could be picked elsewhere, "But does she budge?" Clive's asking the question as though it isn't rhetorical, as though Steven (who is by now drawing thin breaths and seems compelled by the far wall) might verify the unbudging status of Mrs Sergeant. I know Clive's impression of this Mrs Sergeant is for Steven's benefit, but I'm his sole audience member, watching Clive stamping his foot while Steven's eyes roll, waiting for the show to end.

"No use trying to get out of this one, Steven, she says she's lost her boy Lawrence to doolally la-la land again and wants words with you."

Lawrence? I remember the name but can't place it ... Lawrence ... I sift through the years to catch the face—it would

21

have to have been that first year—at the chippie, yes, I can see him now, behind the counter—Lawrence … I don't do myself any favours by saying the name aloud—

"Friend of yours is he?" Clive asks me, a snort demolishing the question.

"Eh, Stevie," Clive says, a finger discovering his lower lip, "you're not in some sort of a pickle are you?"

"No!"

"Because if you are—"

"I'm not, Clive—did she say anything else?"

"Nothing."

Steven shakes his head and Clive sucks in his cheeks, rubbing off the concern that had smudged his face, humming over his cards as he fans them, preens them. I can hear Steven flicking his fingers against the last of his hand and try to keep myself from looking up to see him staring at it, through it. His eyes narrow to dim slits that filter me out, screening off everything but the watch he just glanced at, the cards he now folds.

Lawrence. The chip shop. The fish supper. Then went for our stroll, our paddle—

"Sorry, old man," Steven says to Clive, "think I'm going to have to reconvene."

"Recon-what?"

Steven mumbles something about running a little late, gets up and, while Clive despairs of this *gentleman*, I alternate my nine of spades between its like number and suit—nines or spades I ask the card, offering it to each.

"But I'm on a roll!" Clive reminds anyone who'll hear, holding up his hand. "And besides—what about our guest?"

Nines or spades ... always stick with the suit, make a run, greater odds ...

"Come on then, Sal," Steven says, picking up my bag again as Clive storms on. "Gentleman indeed! Easy on you now, boy, but you just wait till the season hits, place'll be packed out, run off my feet I'll be and so will you if you know what's good for you, no such skiving then—that Mrs Sergeant Major call-her-what-you-like and her doolally tearaway be the least of your worries—" Here Clive admits a pause to examine the effect of his warning. With a sad shake of his head Clive turns from Steven's impassive face to me but already his words had been papered over with the Lawrence I remember: a giant humpty-dumpty standing over the fryer—

All the king's horses and all the king's men couldn't—

But Steven could—or seemed to—

"Thinks he's irreplaceable this one, thinks he's indispensable," Clive confides to me. He tuts, gulps his gin, gathers up the rejected cards, and resumes his shuffling and head shaking. I snatch a glance at Steven—replaceable, dispensable—

"You're not staying?" I ask.

"Not just now," he says, barely audible under Clive's theatrical sighs of resignation, slapping down card after card for a game of patience, still tutting, still muttering and then, with a glare that finds Steven and me equally culpable, declaims how he took this lad into the bosom of his heart—goodness of his soul— "Yes, I took the little runaway, windswept and rain-beaten, put the clothes on his back, dinner in his belly, a haven, rest for the weary ... rest for the wicked! The advantage taken!"

The tirade sounds well rehearsed but no less containable for that—it doesn't feel like a performance—no, this isn't how it's meant to go.

23

I'd be lying if I said I looked forward to having to see Clive, but it only takes a day before I'm used to him, even find him an odd sort of comfort, the predictability of his lines, the way he just wants to play host and in the end it's usually me teasing Steven about Clive rather than him me—but there's nothing familiar about this Clive, it looks like he's been rendered by one of the caricaturists from the pier, a grotesque distortion leaping off the page to accuse Steven. "Theft!" he says. "Daylight robbery! ... treating the place like a b and—what do you think you are? Think you're a bleeding guest, traitor off out moonlighting the nights away, no company over cornflakes, defector! Serving up in classy joints till the early hours. Donning some fancy frock with the stirrers and shakers, eh? Strutting behind another counter, eh? Silverware and crystal flutes, eh? Mrs S come in, does she? Brings her boy, does she? Got a cage for him too, has she? And how about another for that twerp in the bowler hat? Ponce! Wouldn't mind seeing him locked up I don't mind saying—Mr Brody my arse—"

"What's Martin ever done to you?"

"You'd best watch it with that one. Can smell it a mile off. Debauchery may go by another name but it's not the clean promise of a crisp pint ... Those wax wings of yours'll be dripping their lusty way into the Channel one of these days! Tragic Man! Tragic fate! I can watch no more!" Clive falls back into his mutter as we edge away to leave, only I hover stupefied before traipsing behind, leaving my host to exclaim the audacity of sparkling tiers on white cloth.

Steven stops at the foot of the stairs, gestures for me to go on before him. I gauge the flight—the carpet's coming away at the sides, the steps are narrower, steeper than I remember, hiding the safety of the landing as they turn the corner. I test a step and, hearing Steven sigh, stop. "Go on," I say. He makes no protest and is on his way back down before I reach the top.

"Left your bag on the bed," he says, giving a glance down the hall. "Key's in the door, just pulled it to."

"Thanks," I say.

"Not at all," he says and gives me a quick nod. I shuffle sideways, pulling myself in towards the banister, holding the rail a little too tight, feeling it rock uneasy in my grip as Steven thuds down.

"Oh, Steven—" I hear my voice chase after him. He asks what and I stutter on, gripping the dubious rail tighter still as though it might stop me stumbling over my words. I fix my eyes on those useless double bows and swing a clumsy baitless rod into the sea, "I—" and then, risking a look up, I see Steven pull back a cuff to check his watch, sure I can hear its second hand ticking faster and faster, propelling the beat with the impatient twitch of its fine needle, pricking out staccato circles round its silver face.

"What?" Steven asks, his raised eyebrows jerking the beat awake.

Tap—

"Oh, it was just—just that—" I try to reel the line in and, with a blind, urgent toss, fling it back—"Just—no—nothing, it was nothing."

"Right—" he says.

Tick—

"Only—"

Only what? Something about leaves on the line. Was that it? I couldn't be sure, but something had been said—unexpected or unforeseen, unseasonal—yes unseasonal, they said—but I can't meet his baffled eyes with this, eyes that required more,

25

decidedly more, than this about there having been leaves on the line—

"No," I say, "it was nothing."

But it wasn't nothing, or not quite nothing—I can feel it, this not-quite-nothing-almost-something, rustling, scratching unsaid.

Steven's fingers drum absently against the banister, his eyes firmer now, flatly giving their final chance before being pulled towards the passage behind him. "Well then," he says, pushing his hands deep into his pockets. He pulls his lips into a smile and, telling his boots that he really must be off, marks out his exit.

As he goes I hear him call out to Clive that he'd see the old man later. "Hah!" comes the gruff reply and the door slams shut.

But—but it hadn't been nothing, couldn't have just been—all I had through, that thing about the leaves on the line landing me with the burning smack of a bellyflop into a sea of smirking titters. Leaves on the line? Leaves on the line! Even I could have done better than that. Oh come on now—no, really, it was just that if there hadn't been, not that I was sure that there had, but if there hadn't I mightn't have got in so late and if I hadn't got in so late then he mightn't have dashed off so soon and then maybe like we had planned—or like I had planned—the fish supper and a stroll and the paddle and a nightcap—wasn't that what we did, how it all went, was meant to go? Not last year perhaps, hadn't quite managed to meet the pattern then, wouldn't have been reasonable to expect it, not when I'd got us off to that bad start—but the year before—well almost—true we had to pare it back a little but all the parts still in place ... almost all—but that first year I'd come down, yes and the second, more or less ... perhaps less—but the first, certainly—only had to see Steven for the beat to stop—didn't even think about it—felt like I was playing truant when we slinked out past Clive, nipped up the next turning—local secret Steven had said—and into the chippie where a great shiny bald red head was bowed over a grease-streaked sketch on the counter propped up with a pudgy pink hand under multiple chins, a pair of bespectacled milky eyes rising up as we went in. It took a few nods and a second "Lawrence, it's me, Steven."

"Steven?" he asked, squinting as he eased his head forward, his eyes unable to range as far as me. "Ah, yes, Steven," and then, bolt upright, flipped over his sketch securing it face down with a clenched fist. "Evening m'boy," he said, unsticking the glass jar of pickled eggs at his elbow to substitute the fist which then opened so that Lawrence could inspect each of his fingers, deducing which would be the most able candidate to mollify the twitch in his cheek: left pinky.

"Evening, Lawrence," Steven said and, teasing with the stock horror of a hand clasped over his mouth, went on with a sharpened tone "m'boy … and what are you hiding away there?"

Lawrence got all shy, then all serious, saying it wasn't yet ready for public viewing—I remember how he kept calling him Stevie, the strangeness of it, Clive called him that too—we'd never called him Stevie, but somehow it fit, suited the softened outline Steven filled more lightly now that he'd left London—anyway, there was Steven—or Stevie—grinning like mad and trying to cover the grin up—never seen Steven grin like that before—well no, of course I had, but not for years. "Oh go on," he said, "this is me—only me—I'm hardly public."

"Alright, Stevie, but only a quick gander before it gets busy, that's all, and this is nothing final mind, just preliminary …" and, having kept his grip round the jar a moment longer lest it should expose him before he was ready, dragged in a breath and peeled the jar up.

"Oh, oh, I see …" Steven attempted. "Very … what is it?"

"It's … what d'you mean *what is it?* It's, well it's a fish isn't it, a fish in a net, look here," he said, tapping an urgent sausage pink index on the counter, "in place of the lobster see, new logo, going for a fresh look, know what I mean?" The tapping index stopped and hovered over a triangular fin, dipping to trace the dank ring the jar of eggs had left.

"Fresh look?" Steven was trying, he really was.

"Yes," Lawrence beamed, Steven's repetition lighting up his milky eyes. "Yes! And that swirly lettering, you know the kind? Yes! All swirls! And besides," he went on in a solemn whisper, "I tell you—and you're to keep this to yourself mind—that lobster was false advertising." Lawrence put his hands up, "Fifteen years behind the fryer and not single lobster up for sale." He made a precautionary squint up at the door and gestured to Steven to lean a little closer, "All strictly between us you understand, all in strictest confidence—that lobster was a marketing ploy." A shy twinkle had crept into Lawrence's eyes, a flicker of pride glittering under his confession.

"And all this time I …" Steven laboured with a show of mock horror again. "Oh Jesus, Lawrence, just give me a small cod and chips would you?"

Lawrence donned apron and hat with an air of ceremony, officially costuming himself for the role. Properly attired, he made a reverent salute: "One small cod and chips."

I watched, almost mesmerised as his cumbersome frame jumped nimbly to attention, fearing for his tiny white hat balanced on that enormous globular head, seeming like a hapless paper boat teetering on the edge of the world, glistening all the more as the fat crackled before him.

"Get you the same?" Steven had asked, turning round to me. If I think about it now, picture myself still just outside a scene I was under no obligation to take part in, the truth is I was probably as transfixed by Lawrence as he was by the fryer, seeming to be watching him as if through a one-way mirror I hadn't known was there until it was broken by the sound of Steven's voice.

"Please," I said, avoiding the eyes prompted up towards me, hurrying to piece together the features of this strange face, their new focus making me feel startlingly visible, a trespasser caught, feeling suspicion in a gaze that was striving only to create an accurate picture of what was standing before him. The straining eyes glazed, blinked, cleared, leaning for Steven as though they needed him to confirm what they'd seen, as though I still wasn't quite real. The reassurance of Steven's nod unravelled Lawrence's knitted brows, helped his pursed lips to soften, a smile given permission to broaden as he turned back to find my face forged into palpable coherence. Sparkling with the satisfaction of his own artistry, Lawrence glanced from me to Steven and back again to fully relish the success, finally resting his eyes on me to ensure I was quite fixed in place. I pulled my arms about me, attempting to substitute the cloak of invisibility stripped by Lawrence's eyes now blisteringly clear of their blind milky glaze.

"Well," Lawrence said with a wink at Steven's rolling eyes, "what have we here? Well?" I looked up at Steven who offered back his useless shrug. "Well?" Lawrence persisted with more excitement than his temples could accommodate. "Steven, Stevie …" I made a final plea with my eyes up at Steven but a blank face left me to fend for myself.

"I'm Sally," I said, hearing my own name from a distance measured by Lawrence's widening eyes, watching myself look down at my toes pointing up in my shoes.

"Sally, eh?" Lawrence said, winking again at Steven, delighted at his discovery and, turning back to me, held out a greased eager hand, "A pleasure to meet you—Sally. So … Sally," he said.

I coaxed my hand over to his and he gave it a prolonged shake. "Well Stevie, you are a dark horse, how have you managed to keep this little flower hidden away?"

Steven raised his eyebrows and gave Lawrence an exaggerated tut, "Lawrence, Lawrence, Lawrence," he said, wearily furnishing shakes of his head with parental disappointment.

"Steven, Steven, Steven," Lawrence went on, but seeing Lawrence's eyes still glinting undeterred Steven said with a sigh that cut clean through Lawrence's glee, "Yes Lawrence. Sally. My sister."

"Oh," Lawrence pouted. "Your sister."

"Yes," Steven said. "Only my sister."

"Oh, oh well," Lawrence said and, with glum resignation, turned his once more milky eyes back to the fryer. "Only your sister," he muttered, tossing in the cod.

Steven's eyes had a silent chuckle as they caught me wiping down my hands on my skirt. I looked up at him with as much of a smile as I could put together—his sister, only his sister. Only. I hadn't quite felt it then.

Only.

Tap.

No, I hadn't felt it then; Steven had returned whatever excuse for a smile I had managed with his crackling grin that invited me into the joke just soon enough and snapped the tap in two. But now, hovering on this narrow staircase, it makes its quick dive into the gaping night looming hollow before me. The tonic had slid down without fuss then, even let me fight to hide a smirk as Steven worked that magic panacea on Lawrence's pout. Steven's grin. Irrepressible, irresistible, a charm, first sheering Only clean away, left His Sister proud of the title, turned next to Lawrence, his second charge. "Really kept me on my toes yesterday," he'd said to him, lifting Lawrence's eyes back up to catch the grin.

"S'pose I did," Lawrence said, another lapping up the tonic. "Yeah, I did, didn't I?"

"Put me to shame," Steven said. "Call me a fool but I'll brave my luck tomorrow, wouldn't want you to think me a coward. This man is a demon player," Steven had told me then, measuring and mixing tones of awe and defeat to bandage Lawrence's pride.

"Well, I don't know about demon," Lawrence corrected, "but I've got the capacity to—well, let's just say I can put this little novice through his paces."

"Met your chess match then?" I'd asked, enjoying my cue.

"More than met my match I'm afraid," Steven told me, asking Lawrence if they could make it twelve as usual.

"There'll be tears before bedtime," Lawrence cautioned.

"But the chance to learn from one of the greats," Steven said.

"Twelve o'clock then—sharp. The witching hour," Lawrence said confidentially, "with a witch's brew."

I looked up at Steven. "White with two sugars," Steven translated. Lawrence gave a solemn nod of confirmation and wrapped up our cod and chips. "It's a strictly teetotal affair— all things considered you'd best have this on me. Now you just make sure you get your beauty sleep." We did our best to feign reluctance at being shooed away before we let caught giggles erupt.

"Card sharp too, would you believe," Steven had said, catching his breath back as we ambled over towards the beach.

"Poker?" I asked

"No. Tarot," he'd said, his face rigid with a gravity I couldn't match.

"Scoff all you will," he said, "but he takes the role very seriously. Every Sunday on the front, gets himself all kitted out, deck at the ready and calls himself Professor Lorenzo, or Lorenzino or something." His face held out a moment longer before the grin escaped again, "Oh no, don't laugh."

"I'm not!"

"Really no, we shouldn't, poor bugger, gets so upset."

"Not Professor Lorenzino."

"He's sort of, I don't know … sensitive, and the tarot thing—well, he's been much better …" Steven's voice and step slowed before he sought and dropped a limp smile, "Don't look so worried." He tried the smile again, "No, he's grand and I'm telling you, just look out for him on Sunday. Everyone goes mad for him, he's practically a celebrity with some of the kids. And not just the kids. Got letters of gratitude from all four corners of the earth eulogising his incomparable skill—lost bottle openers found, exotic travel no sooner foreseen than one gentleman finds himself transferred to Slough—"

Astonishing.

* * *

Astonishing that I hadn't felt it then—

Only his sister. Not until now does that *only* catch. Steven gone and me stalling on the staircase with a cheeky little spider for company—and not so little at that—least it's just a gasp and a flinch with me now—Steven used to laugh at the way I'd shriek and my whole body would catch, like I had to come round from this great terror that mightn't have been much bigger than a penny—"S'not like it's poisonous," Steven would say—as though that was the point ... *Only*. Hadn't caught me before, no, insignificant as it was meant to be, slipped by, forgotten. Must have tucked itself away, a secret scuttling beneath the stairs, monster in miniature, fattening now under a trickster's lens. Oh little Miss Muffet feasting on the curds and whey of sparkling grins and giggles, bright as the pier lights spangling into molten fluorescence, reflections twinkling and melting over the sea, swirling with the chorus of the babbling swarm bustling round the Palace decks. The traffic of bodies had burst as sparks into couples and crowds: laden with victories, jangling with jackpots, and wired on spun sugar, they mellowed in a post-rush trail onto the beach and drifted to forge islands floating gently over the pebbles, shape-shifting, amorphous. Steven and I part of it then, just another nameless isle, bobbing and settling into soft anonymity. Our little island had held that year, would never have known it to be made of such brittle clay, would never have known it might crumble so quick, wandering to the sea's edge, trousers rolled up, teeth starting to chatter as the water lapped at our legs and wading warmed, the sea's murmuring roll blanketed round us, suspending the beat in its breath.

The momentum of an effortless amble had carried words through a playful rally, stingless quips and jibes tossed in light volleys till we slipped into a silence wrapped safe in the curving arms of a wave. The sea's sleepy refrain had caught us up in its cadence, closing round with a maternal embrace, drafting our isle into its blueprint so easily, so simply, we didn't feel the rhythm that held us, absorbed by it we couldn't know it, wouldn't know it till it broke and left our isle flailing with crass platitudes that just nicked a silence taut against the jagged nerve of the pier.

Must have been the next spring I felt it break, felt it break before it began, the rhythm had dropped us, had rolled on without us as it had rolled on before us. Arms folded, it didn't think to welcome us, hadn't thought to mourn us, wouldn't catch us back, wouldn't be caught back. Jerking round lush isles of laughter in pigeon-steps and strides clipped back and stilted, our fluency choked as we tripped through stale banter—our little isle had turned arid then, cracked and gave way, split as it split us to strangers.

It was that babble of mine that did it. Hardened the silence it hoped to break. Me starting on—about our father's birthday was it? Yes, because I'd wanted to talk to Steven about Dad—well, I could hardly talk to anyone else about him—then it seemed I couldn't talk to Steven about him either, couldn't bring myself to, worried how Steven would hear it, didn't know how to put it, because there was nothing in particular, just the way Dad had been lately, barely heard the sighs or thought anything of the closing eyes anymore, but these gaps—between words, between steps, there was this hesitation, picking something up, holding it for a while, bringing it up to narrowed eyes—almost seemed to be wondering what it was for, what it was doing in his hand—or he'd be standing at an open cupboard, pulling out a drawer before he shook his head and backed away from it as though it was coming towards him—and all of it happening in this slowed but jerky tempo, wrenching a little force that couldn't hold—but it was nothing really, no, nothing in particular, so I just talked about Dad's birthday instead until I could find a way to say what I was trying to say but still couldn't and then having to get away from talking about Dad before I lost both him and Steven at once—I must have stopped and started a dozen efforts at some benign subject or another only to tumble into one that turned out to be anything but benign: the boxes. The boxes of all things. Should never have gone on about the boxes like that.

Jarred the way it came out so sudden. Should never have said anything at all. Torturous game of conditionals. Why couldn't I have just said that Dad had been—well what?

Sorry Sally, just not quite myself these days—

Dad seemed to be saying that quite a bit back then—before that it had always been "Oh ... just fine—yes, always *just fine,* everything, everyone, just"—not the sort of thing he'd say— least not about himself, when it came to him it was only ever just fine and nothing else except for what the sigh said—maybe that was what the sigh had been saying all along—

Just not quite myself—

Maybe, but it made the words sound odd put like that—awkward phrases in a new language—didn't sound right—couldn't get used to it—didn't have to now, stopped saying it—least he was still saying it back then, saying it till not quite himself became himself and he needn't say it—yes, least he was still saying it—though he mightn't have said anything at all if it hadn't been for the terracotta in pieces all over the back steps, soil all over the place and him just looking at it, at his hands, unable to gather how they had had the little plant pots one minute and then ... He'd glanced over one hand then the other before he lowered himself down and was on his knees, cupping his hands to scrape the soil up, but just blackening the steps instead. I'd heard the crack and his *Oh God, what* and come outside, but he didn't look up, didn't seem to know I was there, not until I asked if I shouldn't get the brush or the broom or the—

"No!"

So no, couldn't very well say *Oh fine—just—all just—everything just*—no, couldn't—not then—

Probably wouldn't have thought about it so much but that Sunday—it was only a couple of days later—I hadn't been able

35

to get back to sleep and ended up coming down, curling up on the sofa till the light came in and made me feel I ought to do something so started throwing out the old papers we'd let pile up—was almost finished and about to clean up the old milk jugs no one even looked at let alone used when Dad came down, slow then sudden, asking what I was and me saying I was just and him saying who said I could just and now, look what I'd gone and done, he'd have to go through them himself—and who paid for those papers anyway—yes, exactly—so whose were those papers and there were these—these—oh what were they called? What were they—come on Sally what are they—I don't—yes you—coupons! Thank you, coupons and he was— what for?—never mind what—and grabbing as much of the pile as one arm would hold and tossing the lot across—

Just not quite—

No, not quite himself these—those now of course—but yes, still saying it back then—I'd be saying later how I was going down to see Steven week after next, so if there was anything he wanted me to …

"Oh no, nothing, you just have a nice time and—well, say hello to him for me won't you?—and Sally—"

"Yes?"

"Sorry about all that the other—"

Just not—

Wished I hadn't but I had—had wanted to say something about the terracotta and that Sunday with the papers and the coupons—not to say anything about it exactly, not to go making a thing of it—just to mention—but then you couldn't just mention because so what if he dropped a bit of terracotta and why shouldn't he want to collect the little coupons even if he'd never and what did it really matter if he wasn't—

Quite—

And now suppose I'd be wanting to say how he wasn't saying it because at least then, before not quite himself became himself till there seemed little much to be not quite like—just beating on, clocking up years beyond the requisite three score and ten—now that was something Dad would say—least the three score and ten bit—a good innings he'd say—he would and it was wasn't it—or good enough—but no, still beating on—on and—

"Fit as a—eighty-six years young your grandfather was and every day up with the lark, every day till his last at his desk, yes every single—couldn't stop that—"

Heart beating to the drum—

Ticks back, ticks stop—

Last stop! All change!

Never was though—only the last before the next:

There was an old man—

Yes and he pegged it and still had to begin again—

Oh poor old Michael Finnegan—

So if you think you're out of it when a good soldier like Finnegan dusts off the dust and the earth and the ashes—

No, couldn't say—didn't want to spoil things, bring there here … so I'd gone on about the boxes instead. Never learnt. Hadn't sounded like that in my head—things never did—sounded perfectly reasonable in my head. Not to Steven though. Fair enough, he'd been polishing off his cod, polishing off his cod and working his way through his chips—always like that, first one then the other, kept it in order, knew the agenda—only heard me cripple the quiet. We were sitting by the skeleton pier, the silence running on, my mind's eye tightening up a lively skit to cheat the beat's rise, fend off the rattling bait under the West Pier's black bones. Charmed into a trance as I laced its tonic, the infant-mother heard a lullaby as I watched my sketch spring from its frame: sighs dubbed with chuckles and mute voices flown through a fluent script, my ear keen to still lips tuning our lines and, lighting Steven's blank face back with its grin, I found the Sally beside him a smile that fitted, saw limp puppets become players, laughing, sparring, while two strangers sat dumb …

Breathe just a whisper of life into an illusion and how quickly it grows its own beating heart—the scene didn't need my guiding hand to play the part of the sea: casting us back in the rhythm we couldn't strain back, it painted a drowsy backcloth over the ferment, shaming the gloating strobe of the Palace and the glint in the eye of each laughing isle till each dwindled their smug flash to a distant twinkle and there, just a yard or two up from the water's edge, bobbed our little floating isle: Sally not Sal, Sally and her little sticky angel brother chatting birthdays and boxes. Only Steven had been eating his chips.

"And Harvey of course! He'll love that, he'd love it if Harvey came," I said. Steven walled me in with his blank face.

"But you're right he would," I tried to go on but already that blank face had rewritten my words, garbled the fluency that just now seemed pitched so clear. The blank face sent me back foraging again. I made do with the subplot, not much scope but worth a try.

"And I suppose you could always pick them up then," I said, nudging the words along as they slipped back from Steven's "What?"

"The boxes." Don't stutter, don't—"The boxes, you might as well."

"What boxes?" Steven was going through his pockets for tobacco.

"The boxes ..." Steven shook his head a little and started another search, ferreting now for a Rizla. I watched him roll, the boxes ... the boxes, he might as well since he'd be back anyway that weekend, weekend of Dad's birthday, turning seventy next month, always said we'd do something, make up for so many years unmarked, not that he liked a fuss, wasn't one for surprises, liked to know what he was in for, been in the business of advance planning too long to go in for surprises, been selling pensions for over thirty years, knew the wisdom in planning ahead, easy to get caught short ... but a little something at least, be nice do a little something for him, seventy after all, could hardly believe it had come round so quick, still there was time to organise it all, long as we kept it simple, I said, made the invites as soon as I got back—yes, I'd have to do that straight away, people were busy, got booked up—I could ask for a few days off, Steven too, chance to really catch up with the old man, missed having him about the place, never said anything of course, but seeing as he'd be back it made sense didn't it, to pick up the boxes? Wasn't as if they hadn't been sitting there long enough, sitting there in his room gathering all that dust, unsealed all that time—no, of course they weren't bothering anyone, I hadn't meant it like that—

"Then what did you mean?"

"I just thought you might have wanted them."

Just thought he might need them, whatever was in them, never did say what was in them—

"Nothing."

Reels, I'd guessed, reels and one or two bits of crockery perhaps, must want something with them—

"Well I don't."

Lugged them all that way, all that effort, carting them back to London from ... where was it now?

"Oh Sal, does it even matter?"

"I was trying to remember."

"Plymouth, OK?"

Yes, he'd had that year's stab at film in Plymouth. Seemed like a good idea at the time, bit out of the family scheme of things, but still, and he was hardly going to go in for pensions—

"Let him have a stab," Dad had said after he'd seen him off.

Didn't suit as it turned out. Never said much about it, just that it hadn't turned out. At least the cat managed to get his homecoming right, weaving figure of eights through his legs, not asking any questions. Seemed that cat had sat framed in the window since he'd gone. Jumped off the sill the moment she saw him coming. Only one not caught out by the arrival. Unannounced. Suppose Dad wouldn't have minded a bit of warning. Bit of a surprise. Had been out the back, hadn't heard the bell.

"Good to have you back of course," Dad said.

"Don't see what all the fuss is about," Steven said.

"What fuss? No fuss. Good to have you back."

Just hadn't known to expect him, hadn't known a half-decent glow of health might show up at the front door that evening, bit incongruous that glow, bit out of place in that house, a house that did death so much better, a house that kindly requested such decent glows be checked at the door. Audacity of good health. Still, good to have him back.

"Got a few quid spare?" he'd asked soon as I got the bell and looked over towards the cabbie on the other side of the road, hauling the boxes out the boot. "Fiver'll do. Cheers Sal," he'd said as I handed him the note ...

Sal? Had he said Sal? Was I already Sal then? No, he might've said Sally. Sal was still a good few years off. "Cheers Sally." "Sally." "Sal." I try each of them out in his voice as I rerun the scene, watching box after box pile up on the other side of the road ...

"Seeing as you lugged them all that ... seeing as you'll be back in any ..." Even as we sat by the skeleton pier I'd still had one eye on the boxes being carted up the front path, but Steven's furrowed brow saved me from the rest of each sentence. His narrowed eyes on me for a moment before he started battling with an empty lighter. He gave it a shake and coaxed out a weak spark, flaring his nostrils at it.

"This has had it," he said, getting up. "Back in a sec."

Steven couldn't make it back for Dad's birthday in the end, said he'd have to make it up another time, couldn't get away. Probably best—not to make a fuss—Dad never did like a—just we'd always said we'd do something, and Dad had hinted—so unlike him, but what with it being his seventieth, well, seemed significant somehow and he had always mentioned wanting to get the old boys round—

"You haven't seen them all," he'd said to me. "So long since we've had a good sing-along round the piano, spot of jazz, Pat's wife doing her best, Ella with Pat playing, oh Pat really isn't half bad—not so bad myself come to think of it, but Pat's something, I can tinkle but I'm nothing next to Pat—do you remember Pat?"

"Maybe, was he the one—"

"Shame you never heard him play, real talent, course the old piano hasn't been touched in years, we'd have to get it tuned."

"Steven and I can see to that," I'd told him, "of course we will, we'll see to everything."

Left it all a bit late in the end. Probably best. Never did like a fuss and really, what was seventy years anyhow?

Couldn't have been much more than eight first and last time I met one of them, one of the old boys, never did catch his name though since he was halfway through a bite of cheese and pickle when he introduced himself, but it might have been Pat, wasn't playing of course but then it wasn't really time for that sing-along what with everyone milling round the back room after our grandfather's funeral—this was Dad's father, could only see him as I always had with a pipe and a paper in Regent's Park, a picture that would have been taken before I was born and let me mistake it for memory—all murmuring and refusing to take a seat, doing their best with the sandwiches. Yes, that could well have been Pat bending down as I stopped with the platter, only guest willing to sample a second triangle. "Mind if I ...?" It's not like I was such a shy kid—come think of it, probably would have saved myself a lot of trouble if I had been—but I couldn't find any way to answer this man who might have been Pat so I just stretched the tray up a little—or maybe I was trying to somehow compensate for my height—not quite sure where to look, my mother's voice in my head, telling me not to stare—

It's rude to stare—

Don't stare, I told myself, pleading with my eyes to take themselves off the nail-less thumb of his hand that was just then taking his glasses from his breast pocket, but they insisted on following the thumb while he sent a careful gaze over the rows of triangles. "I must say," he said, picking his triangle, "this one looks particularly good," and nodded as he chewed to confirm the discernment of his choice, "jolly good ... and would I be correct in my speculations that you are the young Sally

Brody I've had such glowing reportage of?" Sally Brody. How nice! How nice to be called by my full name.

Didn't think then how I owed my delight to an accent gloved tongue, a fuzzy ear, and a hasty pen spelling out new lives for a couple called Brodski just off the ship Dad's grandparents had been so sure was bound for New York only to find themselves in Glasgow—Dad always told that one in his Once Upon A Time voice as if he had never told us before, saucer-round vowels and ribbon-tied pauses, all as if it were our story and not one shared with countless others who'd left their names behind, signing off before, signing up for after—Mr and Mrs Brodski; Mr and Mrs Brody—a shiny new name for a shiny new life—but Sally, or in that moment, Sally Brody, even if he did have to go and say young—bet I'd wanted to say I wasn't that young—be nine in a little while I'd've said, well in six months, but anyway, Sally Brody, blushing and beaming, nodded and then immediately shook her head. "No, I mean yes, yes I'm …"

"I thought you just might be," he said. "Well, Sally Brody, I'm much obliged to you for this fine fare, and may I ask, did you make these yourself?"

Oh how I'd wanted to say yes and had started to nod a nod that wouldn't stop, face tight to bursting with this terrible lie until at last I managed to hold my head still—"No," Sally Brody said, "I didn't make them, but I did cut some of them"— and that was true! I really had!

"And very well cut they are too," he told me. "Yes, yes, I can see it." He was studying me from head to toe and back up again—

What? What could he see?

"Yes, there's a bit of your father in you, quite a bit."

Oh well, that was alright, just caught the bit of my father in me, didn't mind too much about him catching that.

"Yes, about the ears and the chin and a speck or two of your grandfather, just a speck mind."

Only a speck? Where? I'd never seen much of him, at least not before he'd had what they all called his turn—at least they had a word for it—never would have a word for what happened to our mother's father—or his brother—always be trying to find it though—one tongues and ears would allow—

"Ah, that was a good man, your grandfather, a very good man, God rest his keeled over soul."

"And was he—is he—is my father like him?" I'd asked, sideways eyes, gathering courage, spying just what they never meant to see—Dad's head over his interlaced fingers, thumbs going round, head and hand made to bob up as his shoulder was patted by all these people I'd never seen—a woman had glued her lips to my cheek a little earlier, wishing me a long life—I hadn't liked that—still don't—and for a minute at least, eight was much better than nine and Steven had been right all along about Peter Pan, better we stayed five and eight forever and none of us ever ever die—

"Ah, your father, not quite the same, quite as good, oh just as good, but not quite the same."

Oh.

"You see, thing about your grandfather—"

Yes, yes? What thing? Didn't dare ask, but desperate—desperate!—to know—What was the thing about my grandfather?

"Well, your grandfather always had a sparkle in his eye and a grin on his face. Bit like that little mite over there," he said, looking towards a sparkling, grinning little sticky angel boy, soon to be sent to play in the garden lest he damage the general mood, all that grinning and sparkling was getting more than a touch indecent. "Yes, just like that," he said. "A sparkle and a grin just like that."

Grin that skipped a generation.

* * *

"Another time," Dad said, "I'll get the old boys round another time."

"Course you will," I said, eyes on the vase, trying to counsel a drooping tulip.

"Best be going on up then," he said. "Best be getting going."

"You don't mind me leaving all that then?"

"Course not, it is your birthday after all. Sure I couldn't get you anything else?"

"No, no, best be going, just have this and be off up," he said, swirling the last drops round a birthday glass of red.

"Well then, cheers."

"Cheers," I said, raising my empty glass a fraction off the table. Dad nodded, his hands on the table, readying himself to get up but just kept on nodding, not moving from his seat until he heard the faint creak down towards the kitchen.

"Aren't you coming up yet?" the bodiless plea from the last step. "Can't you come upstairs?" It edged a little closer, "Please come up, you said you'd come upstairs."

I scraped a nail along a congealed trail of gravy. Up in a minute, Dad said as my mother's face appeared at the door. She'd stood there for a moment, eyes grazing on the empty plates. "All finished without me," she said.

"Yes, all done," Dad's voice flat, brisk, snagged. "Up in a minute."

"Seventy," my mother said, edging away, "I suppose that means I shall die soon."

Dad began to get up as my mother's footsteps died away, stopping once he was almost upright and sat back down, staring over my head at the wall opposite, his eyes vacant, face and body seeming immobilised by the effort until dozing habit woke with a start from an untimely siesta, jerked his nod back into motion, and set him back on course, an empty urgency that pulled him up, pulled him on. "Yes," he told the wall, "yes," and after a final, automated nod began the robotic plod out the door.

I listened to the old engine motoring him up the stairs, shifting that body through and on until he completed the daily circle— remarkable that body, persisting on regardless, just beating on, keeping on, keeping on and at it. Died the second death a while back but on the body went, held up by habit, just had to wait for the engine to flag now, let the body catch up, let it fail, let it go.

* * *

To room five then. Been stalling long enough—as though that might keep waiting eggs from hatching. Find them creeping out from under the skirting, wheedling through the cracks in the walls, nesting beneath the sheets. Quickly I'll have to pull them back—sharp yank like an old plaster, slow peel's never anything but agony. Roll my eyes at my own fear. Still scared of spiders, still wears double bows. Oh little Miss Muffet.

46

Oh Little Miss Muffet who never learns, who babbles away about birthdays and boxes while her brother works on his chips, who should never have gone on, never should but never learnt. Brought city to sea with that babble over the boxes. The city, the avenue, the beat. Brought them all. London to Brighton. Surcharge for excess baggage paid in full with the boxes. Pinned him back in the skin he'd taken such great care to shed, shed somewhere along the M25. Flinched at the very word. Little wonder. Be flinching no less a year later with that hello I'd give up too quick ... no hello from Dad for Steven to flinch from this year. Still, however I replay last year, however many variations on the theme I try, I could never have said—didn't want to spoil the lovely time we were having—would have been having—

Crafty little weaver. Least I've been warned this time, but then I never did—no.

Oh come on now, Little Miss Muffet, that will do. Summon the feet to take the last steps of the flight, to cross the landing and close the door behind you. Mustn't get caught loitering.

Start that shuffle towards night then, its jaws waiting to snap shut in time with the door, swallow me down into its pitless gut of sleepless hours. Empty, waiting. No, no—not quite empty: I'll find those first hours wrung through with the echoes of those still lush, still laughing isles and, sleepless too, the flash of the Palace lights still darting, still dancing, spiralling and seesawing, jumping through the yellowed blind unblurred; then one by one I'll find each hatched egg waiting, crawling into clusters, secret army of the night, marching to the beat. Not empty at all—and my bag of course—my things ... lay out my things. Things. Hardly plural now. Handful if that. Handful rolling around a half empty case. All been stripped back, had to, easy enough to scrape myself down to a handful, down to the noncommittal, the anonymous, things that say nothing of me—hairbrush, toothbrush, a book I won't read—been reading the same line at least three weeks, words scramble soon as my eyes meet the page, won't go in, refuse to speak—handful of token gestures thrown in with whatever had just come out the wash—that and the double bows, had never gone anywhere without the double bows—and the arachnophobia always keen to tag along—very persistent, can always count on it to hold out. Pity there'd been no call to take the passport out of the side drawer, would've been nice to have something so official on me, some sort of evidence of myself—be numbered, located, named in full—make me a little more definite, even with my face bleached out by the light, did away with features—but then I should be used to that, mirror in the hallway of our house is a daylight vampire, drinks us all dry save Steven, always such a shock to catch sight of myself with a drop of blood still left in my cheeks, never seems right, painted on somehow— who's that? Someone else's face looking back at me now from the spotted oval that had observed, unmolested, the spring clean endured by room five: my mother's father's eyes meet and match my own—his brother's too then, I suppose—eyes just bright enough not to be dull seeing a face just large enough not to be small, just pink enough not to be pale—still, the one in the passport is much more in keeping, never been any call for it though except for that trip to Vienna—five days that were going to be the start of something or the end of something and turned out to be neither, but no—no call for it other than that—think the bank might have asked for it once, that was all. Still, I've got my handful. Good to be able to strip it all back like that—not much room to spare, what with the beat: stripped back, scraped down, emptied out—empty as the hours, room left enough inside for ghosts unburied, still trying to find their way home— still wandering, still waiting—room enough to make me know, make me see—not mine to know, not mine to see but still I—

Same eyes as Daddy, same eyes as you—

48

Make me hear—ghosts don't need flesh to hold on to me—hadn't needed flesh to clutch the infant, taunt the mother, the good infant-mother: empty Sal from Sally and Sally from Sal, empty me out to fill me with the beating of waiting and not waiting, fill and fill till I see, till I hear—till they make a living witness of me.

Same eyes as Daddy, my mother used to say to me—the infant-mother too: infant bleating, mother speaking, coming into my room in the middle of the night, the good infant-mother heart-wrung baby gibble-gabble meshed in big mamma coo *ayme-eye-a-da-ee-ayme-eye-a-yoo*—

Two, three, four in the morning I'd hear her, she'd be sitting at the end of my bed, knees up to her chin, mother rocking herself the infant, shushing herself, infant and mother wrapped tight into one, beating. All the day's fire out. I'd be pretending to be asleep, but it was never until I got to school, buttons done all wrong, and my head fell on the desk—*same eyes as daddy-ayme-eye-a-yoo-*

My cousin Melanie was the only other one with those eyes but she got to keep hers behind glasses thick as her fringe—had hardly thought about it, not really, couldn't—but then, just to see Melanie coming out the Tube that day at London Bridge, to know right away it was her—everything else in a different key but Melanie just the same. She'd pulled me into this hug, so tight and sudden—I had to come round, she said—

"Say you will—Mum would love that."

"You're still living in—"

"Yes, God, awful isn't it? But London …"

Brought it all back, made it vivid again—Melanie, Claire, Aunt Vivienne, Uncle Rupert … Go round, I couldn't could I? See Aunt Vivienne? *Mum would love …*

Last time I saw Melanie was when she came to the house with Aunt Vivienne and took away all my mother's father's paintings—portraits, mostly of the same man—my grandmother said she couldn't stand the sight of them—or rather, that they couldn't stand the sight of her—

"How dare they! All those eyes on me as if I owed them something."

Didn't learn until later they were all of my grandfather's brother, all done from memory—my mother looking at the blank spaces on the walls where the pictures had been as though they were still there, seeing her father in the uncle she'd never met, seeing me in them too—

Same eyes as Daddy, same eyes as you—

As though she'd known her uncle, as though having all those paintings of him brought him out of hiding—that was all we knew, Steven and I—that our grandfather's brother had gone into hiding with his wife and daughter in the summer of 1940 and that our grandfather, every step of the way home, pictured them all going through their front door together—only the front door wasn't theirs anymore and, instead of the brother that was meant to be outside it with him, there was this woman telling him to get away in a language he could understand but couldn't speak—a young girl had come out then—

"Anna?"

Was that his niece? So like his brother's wife—but the woman, stunned for a moment, yanked the girl back inside and the door my grandfather had imagined for so long was slammed shut.

Realise now what those scribblings on napkins and bits of paper must have been—faceless faces and doorless houses—always be waiting outside, always be looking out for the same man, the same girl—what's that, who's that?—Steven and I always wanted to know, wanted to look and just as our grandfather would tap the table our grandmother would snatch up the biro or the pencil and the scribbled scrap and stuff it up her sleeve or into her blouse—

"Now no one wants to hear about any of that, Bernard," she'd say—herself a mistress in forgetting since she'd arrived in London from Vienna in 1938 to stay with the wiser than wise Ms Cox I would one day hear so much about—the heel of our grandmother's hand remarking her words against the back of our grandfather's head, wondering where that kiss for grandma Clara was—

"Hmm?"

—as Steven wrapped himself round our grandfather's leg and Dad down just in time to tell Steven that if he didn't let his grandfather have his leg back he wouldn't be able to get him home—

Same eyes as Daddy, same eyes as you—ayme-eye-a-da-ee—

Steven must have remembered Melanie—sure he did—

"You know I've got a memory like a sieve," he says whenever I start trying to piece it all together—trusty half laugh trickling through—or a fish—whichever of the ready-made stock is closest to hand—either that or seems to be tuning a different frequency, my static gibberish scratching beneath—like that when I asked him about that whole thing over our mother's father's arm—Steven was the only other one who was there—he'd seen it too—seen our grandmother stubbing a cigarette out over those marks—"What are they? Numbers? What for? Why aren't we allowed to draw on our arms too? It's not fair and everyone else's—"

"I don't care what anyone else's—go and wash it off this minute—"

We used to try and guess what the number was for, it was always there every time he rolled up his sleeves and set to work inspecting his collection, it must be important, maybe it was a secret code, maybe he was a spy—

"I'll ask Melanie," I'd told Steven, "or Claire—she's older—Claire knows everything."

"What are you two whispering about?"

"Nothing."

A blurry blue scar it seemed to us, not the number that replaced a name, displaced a life—

"There now, Bernie dear," our grandmother had said, giving back the arm that hadn't once flinched, almost detachable the way it was passed over and back, "all better now"—and Steven looking at me and me just trying to look at anything but and hearing my grandmother saying "All better, all better, no one come and take my Bernie now" and later my mother asking asking, "What happened, what happened?" and my grandmother trilling, "Just a little accident, just a little—" and me and Steven not saying not saying because our grandmother had said and so we said: *just a little*—

Steven must remember—so small then but he must—

"Sal," he asks me, "why do you always have to be so—"

"What?"

Be so what? But, of course, I know.

Eight fifty-seven. Watch must have stopped. Must be gone ten by now. But the red lit numbers on the clock by the bed agree without a flicker that nine's still lagging, even gives me an extra three minutes. Very generous to be handing them out like that, just showering them around and more to spare, spare time, free time—yes, all free of charge, Time's treat, footing the bill tonight he says, go on, drink up, drink your fill, all on me, top you up can I? Why not? On holiday after all, Time stops for a break by the sea, just pack up your troubles in your old kit bag and—learnt that one off Steven, well, learnt the words at least, sang it all the way back from Cubs and kept going till bedtime, chirruping away over the beat, couldn't drum through a ditty like that. My old kit bag, left my old kit bag on the bed. Start making myself at home then, just while nine's still catching up, give Night a chance to build an appetite. Not ready for me yet. Content to make do with the day's leftovers, enough there to sate the first pangs—be fine pickings too in the after hours scraps strewn over the pavements once last orders get knocked back and the last pub glow dies, catch almost too easy in light fare as Time comes to sing the way home, a song for company to carry you on and staunch a queasy belly, hum the way through forgotten lines, chorus on repeat till the front door appears, just stop to piss up the ally and kick the stray cans—who moved the house? Sure it was here, ah next turning must be, yes this looks right, soon snug, slight wretch, one chaser too many, no matter, key's in the door, curl up now, warm or wasted, sleep it off, dreamless, no matter, all be pieced up by morning ...

Fine pickings indeed, the very finest. Be hours yet before Night hungers for me—Best of Brighton still to sample, no need to close in yet, quiet now, don't scare the prey, lay the bait and slither back, tummy down—Night's a well practised huntsman, knows to wait; limber up and tease the palette till Brighton's Best is done, time then and only then to feast away till dawn. So leave the Little Miss to lay out her things, to make herself at home, home sweet home—home, where the heart is.

Heartbeat, drumbeat, deadbeat.

Home sweet home, home safe, home sound, safe and sound on her tuffet sits Little Miss Muffet. Yes, slither on back and leave her be. Not a squeak. Not a sound.

Not a sound. Wasn't a sound when I closed the door. Must have known I was on guard. Know that game—the mute click shut, not a squeak out of the hinges either. Clive must've just had them oiled. All part of the spring clean, the spring polish—like Clive said, this wasn't just room five, this was room five *transformed*. Must be how the clock found its way here—might not be new but it was new to room five, its very own timekeeper keeping holiday time, keeping tabs on leisure, on pleasure, clocking all the fun. And oh, what fun! To be beside the seaside, beside the sea … House property. Don't touch. Keep sticky fingers for sticky buns. You've been warned. We don't like a scene. Small print writ large. Large, loud, and clear. House policies. House Rules. Information provided. House Bible can be found in bedside drawer. The New Testament, In House Revision, ed. The Management, Brighton, 1999. Please handle with care due to tenuous binding by means of paper clip. Firm but fair. Breakfast served between seven and half past, we regret late arrivals cannot be admitted. On day of departure kindly note fee applies on failure to vacate room by ten. Smoking, torch bearing, candle lighting, and all other activities suggestive of pyromaniac inclinations—including pyromania itself are strictly prohibited. Surfaces HIGHLY flammable. We apologise for any inconvenience caused. Attempts at rearrangement of in-room accessories will result in penalty at management's discretion. In event of fire please exit via door. Do not use window. The window is not, the management repeats not, for use as an exit point. Your cooperation is appreciated. Complaints unappreciated. We hope you have a relaxing stay. Warmest regards. Do come again soon.

Hairbrush, toothbrush, book. Set them out one by one on the bed. Implacable, silent. Imposters all three. That's it besides a couple of changes of the daily uniform; beat and the bows unpack themselves: my things. Leave the rest. Something for later. Always good to have something saved for later. Just set these in their place—book in company with the In House Bible, choice of bedside reading, muster a little nocturnal zeal while Night's still out on his rounds. Be good to have the chance to brush up on guest house law, help discipline the feet not to mention the mind—must keep the feet in check, liable as they are to being put wrong ...

Watch your step now, keep off the grass, do keep to the path, take care to mind the gap, potholes ahead, we can't say where, your guess as good as ours, potholes, pot luck, chance of a lucky strike—no? And again. Third time perhaps. Third and last, you know the rules. What missed the mark? Bit dark to see? Remember now, it's out after three. Aw, pity that. Sorry kid, game over, it's all above board on boards like these. Above, we said above, above not over ... oh, oh dear, there goes another, what, didn't think you were the only one? Right then. Socks up and buck up. We're waiting.

Two minutes past. Nine had been and gone then, oh yes, striding on it was. Steven and I would be having our stroll by now—our stroll, our paddle ... quick glimpse then, while the blind's still up. Yes, there they are, of course they are, still lush, still laughing. Lush and laughing, little floating isles, floating on without us.

Oh how time flies when you're having fun!

Last look. One last look with the window open, just a crack, just to let the air in, steal a laugh off the breeze—quick! Catch it before the echo falls, their laughing echo, falling, rising, falling. Again and again plays that elated crescendo, forever repeating the overture's promise, again and again it rises and dies, a perpetual return to begin, the last laugh never played.

Laugh? I nearly died! Laughed ourselves sick! Ah, had to be there I s'pose.

Lush and laughing little floating isles, laughing on, floating on, on and on without us. Not in on the joke this time, missed the punchline—

You wouldn't get it. Had to be there, see—

Five and eight, dizzy with giggles, six and nine, seven and ten? Maybe. Eight and—no, too grown up for little sticky angel boys, starting secondary, proper C of E, learnt how to say the Grace of Our Lord Jesus Christ and everything—

Roses are reddish—

New uniform, new best friend—

"Can't I play?"

"No!"

Learning to cut laughs in half and keep a half spare, Steven caught up quick and got better at saving them than me—

Breeze coming in a bit sharp now. Bit through the crack. Should've kept it closed. Gone and let the chill in now. Little point in pulling down the blind, hardly masks a thing. Best leave it up and play along—

Yes! Come on, come on, it's time to play, playtime at the Palace. King and queen for a day, all the fun of the fair you'll have, come on, fair play, fair's fair on this fairest of grounds. Can't lose, honest—we're playing with an open hand. Honest, open, it's time to play so play up now and play the game, everyone's a winner. Every number wins a prize. Odd, even. Even Stevens. Super, Star, bonus, take your pick: it's fun all year here on Brighton Pier.

Rising, falling, rising.

Nothing new in an open hand. All there, every one, face up on the table. Not that an open hand ever changed the score, still hours yet. Hours face up glaring. No courtesy, lingering on like that. No rush then, knows where to find me, meet Night back here. No harm in going down then is there? Go down and join the merry band—

Brandishing his baton the merry drum major keeps merry time, keeps merry feet marching and marching feet in line—

Our mother's mother knew all about merry bands, had liked to tell us about the one that marched on merry, marching to the beat of a merry drum major beating to keep merry time—

"Oh, the merriest," she'd said, "the very merriest—"

Helplessly, hopelessly, haplessly merry!

And while they were marching merry through the streets our grandmother was on a train—

"Go, you must go—quick, now—"

"But what about you and—"

"Now there's a good girl—"

"But—"

"It's all arranged, you'll stay with Ms Cox and we'll—we won't be long—your father and I we'll—but go, now before—"

So our grandmother did. She went. Left Vienna, got on the train, made her way to London, to Ms Cox and while she made her way they were marching through the streets her parents and brothers would never leave, streets she would never return to but always be on her way back to, streets she would try not see as she sat on that train, as she arrived in London, as she sat waiting with the Ms Cox I would come to hear several versions of—they were on their way, our grandmother knew, was sure, her mother had said and if she'd said then—yes, her parents, her brothers, on their way, any moment now—it was always any moment now: they would always be on their way and she would always be on hers—

"Identification. Papers."

"And you are, madam?"

"Madame! Madame!"

My grandmother was no madam! Certainly not! She was madame—or would be but then, she would tell me, eyelids fluttering over the tear that refused to well, "I was a mere mademoiselle."

Left swing right swing, keep those marchers merry, swooping, swerving, keep them on their feet; enlisted, conscripted, and marching merry, enlisted, conscripted—feet wound by the baton, bound to the beat: wound and bound and marching merry, wound and bound, what a wind up, what a wheeze! The merriest of batons makes for the merriest of feet—

Yes, I might go down, just for a bit. Go for an amble, a wander, a paddle, maybe leave the paddle but go for an amble. This chill though—felt it on the way too, be alright, just button up. See Steven for that nightcap of course. Slip out for now and get some of that air, get some ground under my feet. Have to speed up a touch though if there's any chance of getting past Clive without another round, never get out if he catches me dawdling—brief pause then and a quick dart through—careful at the door, bit on the heavy side, pull not push, hinges might go telling tales—bit of luck and chance Clive's already out cold from the gin, either that or stone cold—

Never—he's still going strong and not merely still standing but pacing, pacing with head bowed, hands clasped behind his back, marking the borders of his territory, marking out his patch, pausing only to consult the ceiling and share with it an anguished "O!" before returning his eyes to the floor and resuming his course. Watch from the threshold. Gauge the hurdle: pace, pause, repeat. Surveillance or reflection? Reflection, yes, period of quiet contemplation. Mustn't interrupt—fatal as waking a sleepwalker. Stop to consider—no, no dawdling. Eyes on the door, don't look left, don't look right, just—too late, Clive's caught my feet. He sniffs, steels my name into a reprimand, repeats it.

"Evening, Clive," I say, offering the greeting to my feet and practising the nod and the smile on them to make sure they're fit for reception, the smile still twitching at my feet for a moment before I can reach it up high enough for Clive's scrutiny. I wait under assessment.

"Well," he begins, widening his stance and hooking his thumbs under his belt, "well now, I'm supposing you've just come down, I'm supposing—on account of my tendency to suppose the good in all—to suppose and not to suspect—that you have just at this moment come in search of a cosy chat and a quiet drink, perhaps even a heart to heart with Uncle Clive? Supposing you, the weary, lone traveller come in search of a word of comfort, a word of wit, a word of wisdom, the sort of hospitality money can't buy and, supposing no less, I might supposition that you haven't just been standing about, haven't just been hovering around, having a laugh on Uncle Clive, spying away, sneaking up, trying to test an old ticker, because I can tell you, if you were, well—"

It's not until I see the stern mercy of Clive's nod that I hear what I must have meant by the fraught incoherence that has just jumped from my throat (a jumble of no/of course not/I would never). Clive's eyes soften a little as he releases a thumb to rub his temple—

"Of course," he says, "a girl like you wouldn't have been standing around then … not too long anyway—I swear blind I've only just come down this minute and he scans me again just to make sure but then, halted by the sight of my collar, he mimes a tug at his bare neck and, pulling his tightened fists together at his chest to indicate the offending articles, jabs a finger first at my scarf, waves his hand up and down from shoulder to hips in disgusted recognition of my coat, a throbbing temple ensuring there's no room for ambiguity in his displeasure. He concludes with a thrust of his thumbs back under his belt.

"Am I to take it that you, *my dear*, are off to gallivant round the insalubrious streets of the reckless night, cavorting and frolicking and …"

Never quite thought of myself as a gallivanter, or a cavorter, even a frolicker for that matter, seems almost complimentary. I smile an untwitching smile.

"And grinning like that!" Clive says. "Take me for a fool?"

The guilty smile is quick to prove its remorse and, having wiped the uncustomary calm clean off my lips, I find a suitably repentant note, "Just a breath of air," I say. "Just thought I might pop out for a little air."

"Air? There's plenty enough air in here."

Sin of omission: insufficiently repentant.

"Six hundred square feet of air right here," he says. "You can have all the air you want. Six hundred!" Clive's been measuring up, squared up all six hundred of them and not a breath taken. "Not a breath, not a pew, not a pint." Clive gives a defeated sigh and sits down to his gin, raising his glass to eye level, "Six hundred," he tells it, "a modest kingdom, but kingdom none the less, six hundred square feet fit for a king," and shakes his head as he takes a sip, circling the glass round one of the six hundred empty square feet before him. Without taking his eyes off his gin, Clive flares a hand in my direction, "Another disloyal subject, another lost." Where or what I've been lost to Clive doesn't say. "My subjects!" he cries. "Whither have they gone? Wherefore art mine kin?"

My feet rock from soles to sides and back, debating how they might carry me to the door while Clive mourns his empire: "Here be I, sitting in the face of ruined glory, alone to sweep the wreckage, to slog away in the aftermath when all have fled." He finishes his gin, freeing his eyes to flare up with his hands: "Go off with you then, off into the night, off on the razzle, off to paint the town red."

Right then ... but he's not quite done—"... to think, room five, all polished and spruced in anticipation of your arrival, but no, not enough for a lady of the night. What more can a man do?" Waving off the defence I fail to supply, Clive warns me of cheap thrills and pills and a strange bed, another pill popped in the morning—morning I'd be lucky to see, he says—to put off the bun in the oven ... "But don't expect Lady Luck to offer a helping hand to the lady of the night with your face down in the gutter."

Protest is futile, but my effort at another smile is little better. I'm sure I'll never be granted leave but, as Clive's voice begins to sound as though it's resigned to trailing a grey descent, I reach for the door handle, a cautious hand only making it more conspicuous—

"Sally!"

I prepare myself for a night in with Clive—fine, this will be—but he's thrusting a pair of gloves in my direction, invigilating till I've put them on, his own chest puffed at the sight of my outstretched hands and then, lest he should seem to be condoning my leave, adds "Something I suppose. Will have to do."

"Eh, Sally," he says just as I'm out the door. "That Stevie of ours, he is alright, isn't he?" But I don't get a chance to say one way or another since Clive's telling me not to be such a drama queen, to stop winding him up over Steven, that of course Steven's fine.

Yes, of course.

61

Buttoned up, scarfed and gloved, my lost fingers wiggling in the itchy wool, feeling the light, cool breeze prickle my cheeks and scalp. Air, good to be out in this air, good to have some ground under my feet, yes, good solid ground. I press my soles firm against it. Good, solid ground.

The moon's gone into hiding but the wind's light and leafless branches drape the sky with black lace, just enough of a breeze to brush through the peace, quiver shadows along the dim light of the street. The fervour brewing down by the seafront might be miles not yards away. Across in an open window a man cranes out his neck, leans down to view the motion picture flicked onto pause below. Elbows resting on the sill, his arms dangling limp, he lets the glowing butt of a cigarette fall through the stillness, trembling the snapshot as it taps the quiet ground of his lens. He hauls himself up and, seeing the red tip die, gives a quick nod, a brisk wipe of his palms, heaves the window and slams it down shut: day done. Day done, curtains pulled, lights out: the lens shuttered just before I cross and slip under its eye. Cut from the reel, I follow my path off-screen till my steps fall under the next open lens where the tape runs on, springing me up for view as I creep one house along where four pairs of uncurtained eyes stare out vacant onto the street, eight screens playing to empty seats. My shadow wastes stealth scaling the first storey bricks, reaching to meet shadows cast by leaves strayed from their stems, seeping into them, tangled among them, a brittle few tumbling in half-hearted cartwheels, circling black hands dancing towards the sea.

That Stevie of ours—

The echo of Clive's question—

He is alright, isn't he? Steven, he is—

The question catches me, what Clive had been holding on to me for I suppose, wishing now I could have got away before he'd asked—not that the question wouldn't have crawled up anyway, it's there before I've left London—it's in the Hello Dad always gives me to pass on to Steven—maybe why—no, precisely why—I should have been more careful with it last year—except this time of course there was no Hello to pass on. It's not a question I can answer anymore, maybe last year I might have, maybe the year before ... maybe not—and the first year? I'm not sure I would have believed the question was there for asking, not like that anyhow—better not to ask the questions you're not sure you want the answers to—

No—not that, not now, not out here—here just follow the path of my shadow, no questions, no answers, only watch it lead to two glasses clinking between two candle-lit heads, each dwarfed by a flickering black giant cast towering behind as they sit framed by a blurred eye, winking sleepily between them and the street. Seems eye after eye can barely keep itself open, blinking on the cusp of the first patchy dream, muddling scraps of the day with hazy treasures and terrors, lit vivid and led by an underworld guide with his own curious logic, sprung bright in the dark as they unfold under closed lids and find themselves partnered with an imagined tomorrow—

Could forget for a moment what dreams Night keeps waiting— same again no doubt, same faceless face and doorless house, same merry band of marching skeletons marching onwards, marching upwards, marching to the beat of the merry drum major brandishing his baton to keep merry time—but try telling the sleepless dreamer that—

Only a single eye still on the prowl out here: at number six the vigil is kept by a proud ginger tom—noble subject guarding the hearth—lord protector of his lord and master whose magnificent honour presently slumps face down on his peas, freefalling past dreams to comatose bliss, oblivious to the buzz beckoning only footsteps away, another untouched by the siren's lure, by the hordes pressing on, indefatigable, seething with Night's electrified song. But just as the street reaches for sleep's hand, ready to sink warm in its palm long before Night arrives to take his first bite, comes that shudder that comes just before sleep, that spasm brought by the bright-eyed bedtime sprite—Night's chief lackey's chief delight—who sees the body settling on the brink of sleep, sees the closed eyes twitch, a moment in limbo while they slide from blindness to blind sight as the dark begins to give way and the mind peers through a cracked open door for the first fractured flash of a new weave of old worlds, still busy fussing over its seams—not yet! The sprite chimes, speedily unpicking each stitch, warned by Night not to miss this trick. Without a second to lose the minion of mischief modelled on Puck knows he needs only the merest flick of a fairy-finger to jerk that quiet limb awake. Jolting, the dazed body starts and the door bolts up the dream. Right on cue to burst the sweet lull comes not one sprite but two, two bedtime sprites who'd just themselves been all tucked up and kissed goodnight, had nodded their obedient promise to not let the bedbugs bite, their adorable faces shining pink in the dark. As footsteps begin to fade down the hall the sprites fling back the curtains, their torches flaring under their chins, lighting the giggles that hide in their cheeks, pealing out into the air as the last top storey window swings open, flashing its eye over the street. Strobing their flares first as searchlights, the sprites spotlight their target and gather their arms: tightly bound balls of rubber bands lined up, catapults in hand; mode of attack, considered, approved, confirmed; missiles, inspected, selected; aim adjusted, ready to launch ... Wait for it ...

Bullseye!

Quiet dead with one shot and the bleary eye opposite is thwacked wide awake. The sprites' target lurches up: dazed and glowering, a face swerves out, scowling from brow to chin, "That's two nights in a row you little bastards!" Those giggles are crackling back through them as the sprites close the window and pull the curtains over the glint in its eye. Now back under the covers, all tucked up and kissed goodnight, two shining pink faces tickle with pink peals of laughter, silent pink tickles, tickled pink in the dark.

The street groans as it tosses and turns its way back to sleep, groping for the door to unlock its frayed dream and stumbling over the threshold, falls map-less onto this patchwork of worlds that once again seems new, stitched up by zealous needles with the loose threads of the last.

Not that waking was always enough to unravel the dream. Trespassing into a morning already underway, I can always still hear it, still see it and the clatter of glasses in the sink, the scrape of a knife against a plate; the click shut of a briefcase can only ever just be traced over the dream's landscape of fires and hearts and bones. But then, in the next moment, I see Dad talking to me, see his mouth moving but the sound doesn't transmit. He slips somehow into the background then, the dream's cast of marching skeletons marching past him, still marching on. While their skulls had still held their eyes, they'd flayed their fatless skins to wrap round the hearts they'd pulled out, still beating, the foetuses they'd delivered, still dying, and tossed them into the flames.

"You can have a lift if you're quick," Dad's voice over the fire and the infant-mother coming towards me holding out her burning beating heart.

"I'll be quick," I say.

* * *

Drop of rain was that? The sky answers me with another as I turn the corner and three squealing girls run past barefoot, high heels in hand. Only light though. Light enough for an amble.

Won't be long anyhow. Just nip across and leave it at that. Needn't amble out the whole pattern. The pattern. How did it go? Another time … our stroll and our paddle some other time. Rain be coming down harder soon anyhow. Not really the night for a paddle. Yes another drop, drizzle starting now. Little amble and leave it at that. Just down to the front and back, down to the front and join the merry band—

Never more merry—

If a little more steady—

Oh but what feet would be steady when they could be merry, helplessly, hopelessly—

Haplessly merry! Skidding and sliding as that baton goes flying …

Hearts skip, feet slip—

But the very merriest of batons wouldn't miss a beat—

Caught just in time between squadrons colliding: on blares the siren, on beats the drum, up swings the baton that keeps feet marching on: swings up, beats down, clip-clack, march on!

A voice grunts at me to watch out, huffing its way ahead, jostling my feet a bumbling step on—those feet again, must they really?—the thoughtless pair indulging in a dawdle, putting a swagger in jeopardy, holding up the march.

Really Little Miss Muffet this will not do! Repeat offender we must repeat, you have been told, been warned—

But—

But what? You dare to but! But nothing! On your way if you please— and take that dawdling pair with you.

Them too. Get them on their way, their merry little way, just—

Just nothing Miss Muffet! Quick sharp!

Right, yes, quick sharp, quick march. On their way, on my way, no dawdling, no dallying, no lingering, no loitering—up now, pick them up, up and on, on and up. Onwards and upwards marches the band, the merry band marching, flying the merry flag of fun. But wasn't that a pair there on the brink of a dawdle?

Mind yourself Little Miss, you've no time to ask. Dawdling is reserved for very particular pairs, mitigating circumstances are defined by the board: thieved pockets may be patted and dropped beer cans rescued, wailing waifs silenced and broken heels mourned, the jury—as has been decreed—acquits the pause taken to snap up the fun, yes here you may indeed dawdle as the smile is prepared, the angle is found— all provided of course—it goes without saying—the posers in question assume mask and comportment proper to code—hold still now: don't fidget, don't wince, and you—yes you—stop pissing about— lovely, just lovely! After three, after me and one for the birdie if you please. The who? The birdie! Oh don't be an arse, just smile—and again—and do try to look like you're having a good time—ah yes!— would the camera tell a lie? Golden!

"Well, don't you all look like you're having a lovely, lovely time!" My grandmother, whipping through the pictures I'd taken with a disposable camera Dad had let me have for the bank holiday, smiled fiercely. "Lovely, lovely, lovely!" She'd looked at my mother, "None of you dear?"

"You know I don't like photos."

"Mum *hates* photos," a five-year-old Steven confirmed.

"Quite right too, dear," my grandmother said. "Sally, pass me the scissors."

"Oh mother, don't," my mother began, but my grandmother was already chopping through our faces.

"Photographs only bring back memories and memories are terrible things. When I left Vienna I didn't take a single picture—I haven't the faintest idea what my own brother looked like—can you imagine, dear?"

My mother had just looked away, my grandfather holding up one of his pennies for inspection.

"What's this, Clara?" my father had asked coming in, Steven's face reddening, the cut pictures at my grandmother's feet.

"What's what, dear?" My grandmother's nostrils wide, eyes over my father's head.

But it did look as though we were having a lovely—

Unforgettable! Glorious! Yes, glorious the climb up the golden ladder of fun!—don't look down, I think I feel sick ... Don't stop now, you're on the way up, each glimmering rung a step closer to golden fun! Catch it quick, there's thirty-six to get through! Here, one of you with the rose, without the rose, behind your ear, in my hat, my buttonhole and hah! You didn't really did you? You did! You eating the rose! You ate the bloody thing thorns and all! Nutter! A nutter to crown the golden ladder of fun!

My mother had made scrapbooks when Steven and I were tiny. Not just photographs, but first locks of hair, our names printed in the hatches, matches and dispatches of the *JC*, quotes and letters friends had sent her. I got into the habit of getting mine out the trunk after the first time Dad had to take her to this place he said would make her better. I kept it out for when she got back.

"Put that away," she said.

"But you look so pretty—"

At first I hadn't believed it was her, full cheeks and thick hair, masses of it, trailing over her shoulder ...

"No, put that away, get rid of it—help me upstairs," she'd said to my father, so I sat with the scrapbook in my lap, looking at this woman smiling down at her chubby baby smiling up at her. When I looked in the trunk again the scrapbooks had gone.

"Sorry, Sally," my father had said, "I don't know where they are."

"I have to find mine," I'd said.

"Enough, Sally, I haven't got time for this."

Little Miss?

Sorry, yes—

Are you quite with us?

With you?

The dawdling! Have we made ourselves clear?

Crystal.

So glad—and the ambling, Miss Muffet, take note if you would: ambling feet are not welcome here, no—banished is the ambling foot, exiled is the dithering tread. Not a foot here, you'll see, would lapse to an amble, not one would fall to a dither—feet here know the drill, primed in time to step to our beat—Quick march!

No, no ambling then—and no dithering. Privilege of those who made it across to the decks and on to the shore. Reward for hard labour. Had to be earned. The post-pier amble, the post-supper stroll, dosed up on the day and full to bursting, but still, another drop?

Go on!

On, last legs ambling on, ambling legless, the scenic route.

Not yet time for that amble, threatened the squadrons' pace—squadrons militant with joy, leading this very merry band now surging up towards me, behind me, lurching me seasick between two simmering waves, swelling as each gathers the bodies seeping onto the street, pooling at the open doors, out from dinner, from drinks, trickling seaward from their sheltered coves and bays. Burbling in rivulets, the current swills them down, thirsting for bodies that fit right in their skin, for faces flushed with nostalgia, expectance, still warm, still soft; unquenchable, it drinks deeper, wider, curling its tongue up behind blind resting backs and, gulping them under, whirls them into the rapids governed by Night. Relishing his sovereignty over the tide, Night flings back the crests seething to turn, tearing them rabid up through the shallows to unmoor the last anchored feet and suck them into the storm—feet that in a moment would know not to dawdle or amble or dither, no, such well-trained feet know, once swept up by the storm, to kick off into strut, a saunter, a swagger, and riding the height of that exultant wave, roll on, march on: marching on the merry band, marching masked in their merriest masks, masks delirious with cheer, impervious cheer, masks carved by the serial knife of delight and oh how very merrily does this masked ball of a band march! Whipped on, whipped up, up to the pier and gulped down into the vortex, hurled up to the casino and off for a song: this our merrily masked ball of a marching band singing along to Night's merry tune—

Upstage, on parade, marching masked in their merriest masks, the very merriest of masks, the very merriest of feet, of heels, beaten, battered, bitten upbeat: down beats the baton and up plays the band, up, plays up, up back and on, up to the baton, back to the siren and now on with Night's song: pounding in platoons packed tight, pounding out resounding chords—

Just must must keep keep—

Pounding, resounding—

Thundering on!

The waves of bodies tower into one and thunder over the crossing, storming the front till its roar breaks against the sirens' song. Deafening: chiming in technicolour, the insomniac jingle chants round insomniac lights, blaring a score for the blaze scorching false stars through the starless night, searing the iron sheet of cloud encasing the sky. Just a few bodies caught at the curb, the wave's thin tail folded back, left lapping hungrily behind the wheels hurtling on by, lapping, bobbing, waiting, treading water in the slackened tide.

A gaggle of hens totter to join them, tongues clucking, heels clacking, the still waters bubbling with their spluttering steps. Could splutter on behind. Catch the wave's tail and hope it wouldn't snarl at the touch. Best hold back a little then lest it bare its teeth, teeth of a fat crest rising out of the tail, rising, swelling, spawning a new head, a fanged wave snarling this last body off its back, this last body that didn't fit right in its skin—

But how could this body fit right in its skin? Skin snug round a body would never the ghosts slip under—faceless, nameless, untraceable, without origin or destination—these ghosts couldn't wait for Night, no schedule to stick to—just slipped in, slid out, good enough for them this last body lapping too late to lap so close, this last body that would never board the rising back of a wave, never get ferried across to the front—

Splutter on in a moment then, follow in the wake of that bubbling trail, follow on up to the curb—just let this pair of swans glide through first, gliding the stretch from the Grand, fairy godmother feet hidden under their gowns, gliding up with invisible steps, smoothing the water down—

A man in a purple velvet suit curls an Elvis lip at me. "You local?" he asks.

"Sorry," I say, "no."

He preens an oiled quiff, "Trying to find the Old Ship."

The Old Ship—I know the Old Ship. It's just down, or just back—Steven would have known, easily, if I'd been with Steven—but the velvet suit is already strutting away, sliding between two women, "Excuse me, ladies …"

Waters unsettled again before that splutter had even begun—

If I'd been here with Steven I'd—

Unsettled soon as those swans had glided through: straight past the crossing and vanished upstream, looped out of the labyrinth and left the waters to bubble up with a wriggling child, stamping away on the spot:

"No, it's not fair! I'm not tired—"

"Yes you are, you've had a long day."

"I'm never going to bed! I'm never going to sleep—"

"Oh yes you are!"

"But you promised—"

"I never!"

"Then you're a liar!"

"Did you just call me a—"

"With pants on fire!"

"We'll go again in the morning."

"The morning? I can't wait till morning!"

"Tomorrow's another day."

"S'not, it's forever, you're always saying tomorrow and tomorrow is never the same."

Always tomorrow. Always another day, another time. Yes, another time. Just down to the front and back then, get these feet spluttering on.

"B-R-I—Brrrrrrrrriiiiiiiiiii—G-H-Brrrrrrrrriiiiiiiiiiiiiiiiiiiiiii ggggggggg"

Letters flashing up in turn as the little voice behind sings them out. Must've wriggled free.

"H—T—Brig-het-hut-Mum! Mum! What does that—"

"O—N—" I mouth along as he strings them together, chirping a shrill victory as high and long as his lungs can carry.

"BRIIIIIIIIIIIIIIGHTON! Brighton! Brighton! Brighton— P—I—"

"E—R—"

Fun all year here on—another time. Never really was part of the pattern anyhow. Not since the four of us trundled down for the bank holiday. Twice a year dressed up in the holiday habit. Spent the morning jammed in the traffic and the afternoon breathless in the sun. Always sweltering. Never seemed to rain. Couldn't once you were in the holiday habit. Waited for the journey home at the very least. Good to have it coming down just as we were off, confirmed it was right to be going, watching the brushstrokes of the picture postcard we'd left behind through the back window run streaked, whole set blurring and the sky weighing down over the sea. Comfort of the monotony of it, pattering all the way back to London, pattering over the gasps and the sighs and me and Steven too sleepy to squabble. Home to find the carpet bleeding dark under the leak, but be so snug once we were under the blanket, listening to that drip drip drop into the bucket and the relief when you gave up hoping it would stop, sure of the rain, sure of the feet, not having to work out where to put them, having the certainty of the snug spot under the blanket. Felt warm just watching rain like that and yes, quite sure of the feet, quite safe, couldn't go putting me wrong—only that afternoon they'd come loose from their patch besides Dad's on the Palace decks—had meant to keep them put of course—just wanted to see what the talking telescope was all about, never seen a telescope before, and here, one that spoke!—Never meant to—eyes getting all blurred looking out for Dad's brogues—had to be brogues, always his brogues, brogues rain or shine since some concessions just couldn't be made, not even for the holiday habit—but only all those feet poking out pink and red from their sandals—so many feet but all the wrong feet—wrong in their sandals, their flip-flops, their jellies, horribly wrong pink and red toes rushing past under my watering eyes, watering wide, looking up blind, searching all the wrong faces, pink and red as their toes, blurring together under the sun and having to blink, blink hard against it, that sun too bright—oh I'd never find him! Never, and there I was, couldn't see and—where were they? Off! Yes, they'd be off, already off, down off the decks, off the decks and on the beach, Steven sitting up high on his golden galloper, up high on the carousel, round and round he'd be going, round and round without me—and then it'd be time for tea, always had afternoon tea at the Grand, wasn't bank holiday without tea at the Grand, had to have tea, had to for the holiday habit and there their feet'd be all neat and tidy under the table while mine were all a mess on the decks and then—well, our mother'd say Steven was tired—but he wouldn't be tired!—and pale she'd say and Dad would nod and say how it was getting on, getting late, how really they should have got going by now—going! Yes, already driving away without me! No, no they'd never do that—but they might, they might have to, have to because Steven was tired—

"No I'm not!"

"Don't you argue with your mother—"

—tired and pale and it was getting on, getting late and they had to get—but still all those pink and red and pink and red faces, all rushing past, all the wrong faces—Daddy! Steven! Where are—all horribly wrong, never find my way home, that sun raging down, beams scorching—just as the voice had said, the one on the radio, that one always so jolly, must have been the jolliest voice I ever heard, "IT'S GONNA BE ANOTHER SCORCHER!!! YeeeeeeeeeeesSERIE!" He really was very jolly and put on this jolly twang for the "SERIE! SEEEEEEEEEEEREEEEEEEEEEEEEE SIR! That's right folks, ANOTHER SCORCHER! So slap it on—" and the jolly voice would go on—as if we didn't know stuck in that bottleneck with no breeze coming through—until a whack against the button shut the jolly voice right up since it had gone on being jolly quite long enough and all this jolliness was making our mother ill—as if she wasn't quite sure she'd be sick any minute what with this jerking and swerving and—

"Drive with both hands! My God you never look!"

"Would you like to drive?" Dad asked the steering wheel.

"Well now, that's a cruel question," our mother said, "very cruel, you don't have to always be quite so sharp when I only said to look and was only thinking of the children when you couldn't care less—not about them, not about me, should count your lucky stars but you don't even care—"

"Don't be absurd, of course I—"

"So children you see ... you see—your father," and here she'd catch my eye in the mirror and smile—"your father wants to kill us all"—some concessions would never be made, least of all for the holiday habit ... Nice to have the rain pouring down then and be all snug under the blanket and listen to the leak drip drip dropping and have the feet in place, neat and tidy feet kept put.

Not that it was coming down much now, pavement only just damp enough to glisten. Yes, still only light, only a quiet sheen under the lamps, still light enough for that—no, no ambling, amble had to be earned … another time, yes, always another—

Slip off the wave's tail at the front. Slip off and let the crest roar on, stand at the railings and watch till it breaks. That would do. Be enough. More than enough to be getting on as far as the front.

So splutter on then and quick—quick before those bodies left lapping couldn't lap any longer, bodies left lapping been lapping hungry too long, wouldn't be kept lapping by a last body coming to lap so late—see the wave's tail frothing impatient, already rising, swelling, spawning that crest ready to surge, spurning those wheels with its spray, its snarl saved for their horns daring to keep back the storm, keep those bodies from leaping, darting to dodge between bonnets, daring to stall them, daring to rival that deafening song, the song of the siren blaring, blazing on.

A car horn blasts, jolting me back to the curb: last body snarled off, snarled back, last body left lapping without the hunger to lap, left with those feet snarled into place, their heels that wouldn't clack locked quiet at the curb.

Those feet. Those heels. A cane taps once, twice behind them, tapping a tut against their frozen silence, a tut, a titter, a chuckle and away the cane taps besides a far superior pair that exchange their clack for a clip, a most excellent clip—even, resounding, a superlative clip, quite enviable these heels clipping up to a march, heels of a cane tapping chuckler clipping a safe distance from a most unfortunate pair with no hope of a clip, what hope did they have when they wouldn't even—

But no, not that they wouldn't, it was just that they couldn't—

76

Couldn't or wouldn't, Miss Muffet: those heels don't clack.

No. Causing a racket of a silence. Nothing. Can't get a thing out of them. No way of knowing how long they'd kept mute. Years no doubt. Mute for years and never knew. Deaf to the silence all this time. Trickery of the quiet again—always falling for that quiet. Forgot them under the feet. Easily done while they clocked up all that mileage with the same two steps—forward, back, forward, back—keeping the game up and all quite convincing till I see the view still hasn't changed and then off they'll go, putting me wrong—never know where I'll end up with feet like these, always remembering the trail of crumbs too late—

Handful of crumbs handed down: hand-me-down handful Steven and I had never asked for but had to take, one we'd been given to share and scatter together—help us find a way back, back to the beginning, to that before, and piece it all up from there—see how and where and why—find the beginning to find that end—that before to find that after—find the ghosts their way home to find our own way home—

"Leave it, Sal, just—"

Had promised myself I wouldn't mention Vienna again but just had to ask, just check, did he want to come with me next time? Steven's eyes had closed then and there was that long breath before I'd even finished the question, the turned head and the bite into his cheek getting more and more like when Dad would say he was sure it was never all supposed to be quite like this—heard Dad say that so often it seemed he'd always said it—or the closing eyes and a sigh said it for him—wasn't supposed to be heard—not that first time—

Sure it was all never supposed to be quite—

"Like what?" my mother had asked. "Go on," she'd said, "tell me, tell the children, like what—"

And then my mother's mother la-la-la-ing over it all and say-ing wasn't this all very nice while Dad just got on with getting his coat and his keys and—

Sure it was never all supposed to be quite—

That was maybe the second or third time my mother's father had gone off—

"Don't worry, dear," my grandmother had sung in the no-use-crying-over-spilt-milk voice she'd perfected with tireless prac-tice supervised by Ms Cox, "he always comes back"—and then Dad would be sent out to drive round and round looking out for a man stopping every so often to inspect a possible addi-tion to the miscellany collected in his pockets and my mother saying they had to call the police—

That word—police—coming with the sandpaper scratch of a hissed whisper from my mother, worked on my grandmother like a token dropped into a forgotten slot machine. Her eyes, interred beneath weeping yellow crusts, split open, emerging from their tombs as hard and bright as boiled sweets. She snatched up the phone from the table beside her then and, once settled on her lap, curled a tigress's paw round the receiver.

"No one," she said, "will be calling anyone—"

No, she would not let the police get their nasty hands and have their nasty way—she picked up the receiver—"Bernie darling, is that you? Not now darling, I have guests"—and placed it back, two paws curling round it. "You see," she said, "he's fine—" and here she turned to offer what was left of her eyes, dissolving now into syrupy wells, to Steven and me, "Who wants to be first to give grandma a kiss?" Steven and I mouthed *you* at one another, *no you!*

"Grandma's waiting …"

"Mother, please! Oh if something should happen to daddy—"

"Nothing's happened to daddy—it's just his little game. Now who's keeping Grandma waiting for her kiss? Hmm?"

"Maybe Bernard went to the shops," Steven had suggested.

Even then we had always called our mother's parents by their first names, Clara and Bernard, never grandpa or grandma or any variations on the theme, no matter how much our grandmother valiantly persisted in referring to herself as grandma. Our mother's mouth opened and snapped shut. Steven shrank back.

"You are a clever boy!" Our grandmother's eyes had boiled bright again as she kissed the air's cheeks in turn—"A clever, clever boy!" The angel-imp couldn't help but sparkle without reservation until he realised such cleverness had nominated him as first to kiss.

It would be another fifteen years before Steven and I tried to align our sliding memory of that afternoon, only now it wasn't our mother's father who had gone off but our mother. We'd been sitting in the front room since we'd heard the door go and the walls hold their breath two hours before. I caught Steven's eyes redraw their semicircle from watch to clock to window to phone.

"I think Clara really did adore you," I said.

"Hardly—" Steven was grimacing.

"Clever, clever boy! ... She wasn't that bad—" I said. "She meant well—" Steven asked who didn't. I had looked at him then but he'd dropped my eyes and went to the window.

"I'm not sure what she meant," he said.

"Well enough—" I said. Steven started a protest, saying he never would have said that about the shops—that I must have made that bit up—but I was sure I remembered him saying ... Had he smiled then? I like to think he did, admitting it wasn't entirely implausible … our grandfather might have gone to the shops.

Less plausible somehow was the idea of our mother at the shops. Two hours. Well, no one could say she hadn't warned us—"You know what they'll say," she'd said.

They never did have the chance to say it though since Dad was fairly certain where she was—

Sure it was never all supposed to be quite like this—

Not quite, no. With her raincoat over her nightie he'd found our mother not more than a few steps from where the two of them had picked up her own father fifteen years before: King's Cross station, emptying out her change, asking the attendant when the next train to Vienna would be.

Daddy's little game.

Handful of hand-me-down crumbs to find the way back—to see—so many befores we'd tumble over—so many I'm still trying to find—mightn't have be mine to find but that didn't stop them demanding to be found—of course that day Dad had brought our mother back wasn't the first—the first was somewhere behind that doorless house, somewhere in Vienna, somewhere that might have been home, somewhere that didn't know the beating of waiting and not waiting, of wandering— but that day, sitting there in the front room with Steven, was the end of our before—of mine and Steven's—wondered what Steven remembered—must remember—couldn't ask—not now—tune me out—

"Oh Sal, not all—"

"That again, yes—"

Had tuned us all out—what he'd left, not his, wouldn't see, wouldn't hear—some concessions will never be made, least of all for the holiday habit—

"Oh come off it, Sal," Steven would say to me, say I could just let all that go, that it was their history, not ours. "Walk away," he said, "it's not that hard"—and he said it so well, said it like he didn't feel a thing, like I shouldn't feel a—

Walk away then, just—

But it never made any difference, however far or fast I go the beat follows and every there I get to is never anywhere but Vienna—

Had always thought there was me and there was Steven and then there was everything else—see now I'm in that everything else and being here, coming to Brighton, bringing what he'd left, the beat I couldn't leave behind, that was meant to sleep as it had that first year I'd come down, ruptured the seal between now and then, him and us—shouldn't have come this time, might've taken the hint after what he's said about a day trip—but it was always three days—always—stupid—no, should never have come—and then to think I could stave it all off tonight with my own little amble—feels all wrong being out here—wrong, odd, watched—those eyes on me, feel them all—eyes out here become the eyes in all those portraits, the ones my grandmother couldn't stand looking at her, eyes that might have been in the faceless faces, a thousand eyes, back there, out here, a thousand spinning to stare—oh, they were spinning, certainly spinning—a thousand—more, certainly more!—thousands upon thousands spinning united to stare, bound by this spectacle, this sight—this eyesore of a sight—this sight of a fool just declared with a snarl, confirmed with a tut, this fool just now reproved with the tut tut titter of a cane-tapping chuckler—and eyes had to ask eyes:

Did you see, did you see?

Did I ever! But what choice? Duty of the eyes to endure the sight.

Ah, brave eyes, hardly believed my own—

No? Well, believe ours and what's more, do you know—at least it's been said—the heels of this fool don't even clack.

How very peculiar! Simply bizarre! But how to be sure when its eyes that don't lie, eyes that don't miss a trick? But mouths—can they be trusted? And the ears—were they sufficiently pricked?

Certainly—all ears they were, well pricked indeed and sharpened too—sharp as our eyes, braved the silence as we braved the sight—but oh how brave those mouths speaking the oracle through a thousand lips: a tut and a titter, a titter and a tut, attest to the judgement of the cane-tapping chuckle—

Thousands of lips, thousands of eyes—spinning incredulous, spinning as one, the all-seeing eye, a monocular god, declaring, confirming, reproving this eyesore of a sight, this fool whose heels—no, really?

Yes really—a fool whose heels don't even clack.

Don't?

Won't!

Wouldn't!

Or tell us, Miss Muffet, was it just that they—?

Couldn't!

Couldn't or wouldn't, still had to get them up and out of this glare, step them soundless out of the light. Won't move though, clinging to the darkness beneath—have to get the feet up, can't keep me under this street lamp—lamp hasn't flickered once and here the feet are, taking centre stage in its wide pool of light, thick yellow light. Had the ground under them now, didn't they? That ground I'd gone insisting on, that good solid ground, soles gripped rigid, stiffening themselves against the shudder through the pavement, feel it throb with the lash of pounding feet and pelting rain. Tipping down now. Knew it would. Air been thick with waiting rain since I made that turning towards the front: heavy, unfallen, waiting to beat down, waiting just over the drizzle. Air almost too thick to breathe, air I'd gone insisting on a breath of, insisting when it was thick with waiting rain and staring eyes and then those pounding feet auguring the tower and surge of the next marching wave ... So much for solid ground, end up drenched and hobbling—just as well it wasn't the two of us, both wet right through and cold to the bone, Steven getting all tetchy, doing his best not to stride, not to sigh. Right pair of fools we'd be, cold and wet, paddling about in the rain.

Only it wasn't quite so bad being a fool when there was another paddling beside you, didn't mind the rain so much then, had to admire the perseverance of it, almost comical the whole thing, rain bawling away, not letting up, throwing its tantrum on the water, trying to make a whole drama out of the waves and us paddling on regardless, just going on with that paddle, the ritual paddle, just another pair of fools paddling about in the rain.

Still, just as well. Time to get these feet out of this glare and back into order. Least get the toecaps off stage. Would quiet down in the dark should think, silent as the heels then. Just have to find them a patch between these pools of light, must be one spare under an awning, spare patch of dark, be out of this rain, this glare, settle back now the right side of the footlights—only would have to be braved past those eyes—oh those eyes, those thousands of eyes, those thousands of eyes spinning to stare—

Over on the pier a chain of bulbs swings its maniac seesaw, plunging down, lurching up, its hinges yelping between two of the playground's bullies straddled either side, *Up, up, up!* they snipe over its whine, *Up, yes up! Faster! Higher! Up, up, up!* Swinging, plunging, lurching, jeering those slackers, those stragglers, those heels that wouldn't clack still locked quiet at the curb: *Up, yes up!*

Yes, up and on—but not an eye on me. All seeing sees nothing. Too busy busying round puddles and watch faces, no time for a shameless toecap—besides, had nothing on those patent points—now that was gleam! And that satin pair—gleaming all the way to the ball! Not an eye then—not an eye not a tut not a titter, only the tap tap tap of a light deft cane trusted to see for steps treading blind, feigning faith with a clip, stop-starting before their guide. Hardly hear it now, clip doubtful, muffled as it draws cautious on, faint the way through the labyrinth, lost under the parade now huffing and bustling out of the rain. Yes, have to strain for it—hear it just—there it is: the tap tap of a light deft cane—tap tapping without a tut.

This ground holding up well enough too. Quite firm under the soles. Took the lash unfazed it seems. Heard it all before of course, the pelt and the pound, all slipped down without complaint, down into the cracks of its well-trodden face, fissured by feet that reprinted the tale of yesterday's step, long worn with the stories told in its lines. Good to shuffle over ground that didn't comment, shuffle quite passable over ground like this, ground that would sleep under the dregs of the revels till the morning sweeps them away. Didn't distinguish shuffle from bustle, pelt from pound. Shuffle no odds at all on ground like this—best keep it off those cracks even so, what with it bearing up so well—yes quite passable this shuffle shuffling on without so much as an eye to catch it—but I catch one— eye of a gentleman obediently holding still—all for his own good, or so the two ladies would have him know—and know again—the two ladies now standing before him, presently involved in a fraught exchange of responsibilities, taking turns to attend to the fussing and flustering—simply unavoidable where their gentleman's top button was concerned—while the other suffered the task of providing shelter for three with an umbrella suited for no more than one—the gentleman's hands having proven unfit, being given as they were to drift in and out of sleep, invariably surrendering both themselves and the umbrella to gravity—caught this gentleman's eye quite by accident—very diplomatic though the lid, drooping straight over, didn't much care to light on a shuffle, didn't much care to light on anything at all, just one of a pair wandering off while it could, preferring to avert its gaze from the flurry of fingers burrowing under his chins, determined to conquer this obstinate surplus of flesh, refusing to be discouraged by the glaring fact that no there was no remedy for a collar quite so heavily buried. The gentleman's eyelids droop back for the final tut— the mournful tut, the tut of defeat—and with regret open as each lady is forced to slap the back of a hand against each of his inattentive arms. Forgive the perilous yawn, gathering behind those chins, as the arms concede and take up their tasks; next the heels, implored not to protest, are dragged before they have a chance to refuse, heels without so much as a clack between them, another silent pair on the wrong side of the footlights, the ladies clacking proud either side, trotting on, the two quite restored, trauma of the collar notwithstanding.

Might as well trace the pattern myself for whatever it's worth— not as if I don't know it well enough—the fish supper, the stroll, the paddle—all laid out by that first year—should have been nothing for the years that followed to do but unfold over it and I can always see them unfolding—watching myself and Steven play it out along the lines that first year had set—see the whole thing playing out beautifully—even coming down on the train last year I could see it, see it all going how it was meant to go—quite redeemed the year before—the year before slipping under, remodelled back on to the first—yes, all going just how—at least while I was still on the train it did—no mention of birthdays or boxes—no babble, none of it. No getting round the mess I'd made of it last year with that Hello of Dad's but after that we'd been alright—or would've been if I hadn't started on about Vienna, saying I was thinking of going back,

another trip—would've been better off babbling about birthdays and boxes—said I thought I'd go in September—

"Everyone says September's the time to go."

"Not again, Sal—"

"A bit longer this time," I said, "those five days were …"

I didn't know what those five days were, still don't, but they
weren't enough which is what Steven said they were; more
than enough, he said—

"Not really—there had been all these things I thought I'd—
well there was just such a lot—"

"What did you expect?" he asked me.

He was right of course—what did I expect? That you could just
find a name or two etched or archived or else find some—what?
Truth was I didn't know—I'd wanted just something you could
touch or see, something that would place them, root them—find
a way for the ghosts who'd never found their way home—find
them their way to find my way—Steven's too surely—maybe
not then, seemed he was after another, didn't want to share
this handful of hand-me-down crumbs, following another trail
while I went on the one that was meant to lead back to that
before, that beginning where I'd find the ghosts their end, take
them out of hiding, stop them waiting, stop them wondering—
anything that would lay them down, give them their graves,
their due, still the beating of the infant, the mother, the good
infant-mother, that bleating still beating, still bleeding raw—
the beat of those waiting and those who never had the chance
to wait—those who would never stop wandering: Palestine,
England, America—anywhere but there was a promised land.
They were safe now, they were free. But they never stopped
waiting to be caught, never stopped looking behind them,
always be trying to find their way home—

"I just thought—"

"Yodelling and schnitzel?" Steven said he wished I'd just leave that all alone.

Another of the long breaths then and the closing eyes—of course after that he had to go—something or someone—of course—should've just gone straight back to the guest house then—I'd meant to: do not pass Go, do not collect £200—only I couldn't—not yet—not while how it was all meant to go was playing itself out beside Steven disappearing into the crowd and me just standing there watching how it wasn't going— still, at least we'd had our stroll last year—

"Well, just a quick stroll then, Sal—"

A quick stroll? Would have to add in a half-laugh to the mem- ory of it later—have a half-laugh for us both then on the way to the chippie—we'd have had our fish supper by now of course but it wasn't too late—or maybe just to go past, wouldn't really want to go in, doubt Lawrence would even recognise me—least not without Steven—this turning? Sure it was—no, well then maybe the next—just to pass by was all, if I could know that Lawrence was still there—the Lawrence who knew no other Steven but the Steven from that one year—yes, if Lawrence could be there just as he was, there behind that counter, in his paper hat, Steven might too be just as he was—let me feel the pattern was still there, a part of it still in place, waiting to be played out by a pair who'd only ever played it out that one year, just that once but still it might be there, waiting to be made into a pattern.

No this doesn't look right—no this definitely isn't it—except— was that?—no, boarded up shop front, couldn't be, then why can't I just turn around, as though peering through at nothing might transform it into—

All so quiet—where to from here? Lost my bearings—the street moves beneath my feet, everything kept so far away—just find my way back to the seafront for that stroll—

But what was—

Something round my waist—tight—a hand—tighter—and up my back, clasps my neck—and a voice so close—feels as though it's breathing inside my own head—

"Bed for the night, my love?"

Can't slip myself free—this arm—

Get it—get—

Clamped across my front—

Get—get—

Underbelly rumble of a pantomime cackle—

Run run—

As fast as you can!

Can't catch me I'm—

Nobody—

Nobody? Never heard of—

"What's your problem, bitch? Was only after a good fuck—"

Feet faster, further, have to slip free from the sliding hand and the clamped arm already streets away—are they or is it just the street moving beneath my feet again? Look around—no, but still feel as if—and trying to silence that cackle that echoes in every laughing face—wait a—where the hell am I?—couldn't have got that far—where's the guest house from here—and the sea—why can't I hear the sea? You could always hear the sea— and then oh, thank—

"Steven! Steven!"

Yes that's him! Oh how ridiculous it would all seem now—the hand and the cackle that was really nothing—getting all jumpy and—

"Steven!"

There he is, waiting outside a house, hands in his pockets—he won't mind, I'll explain, laugh how I'd managed to criss-cross the whole of Brighton and—oh! Going in circles—

I stop, take back my last step as a composite somebody—one as good as anybody that might as well be nobody—turns—

"Sorry I—"

And disappears through the disappearing door of a disappearing house.

Well so that's how it goes. Could've been worse. Least I managed to stop myself calling out after all the other Stevens I was so sure I'd seen. No use trying to find my way—have to just ask—

The man who gives me directions is kind enough not to laugh, heels clipping away, cane tapping behind—

What after all—yes, after all that. Had my stroll then. All 100 yards of it, what seemed so far away so close, everything embarrassingly familiar, the chorus, the street, the sea, and all those feet going, heels clipping, clip-clacking—never keep up with the merry band marching, marching on, marching up—

Onwards, upwards must merry marching feet march, the merry band marching flying the merry flag of fun—

Never could keep up—in dreams chasing after, calling but wouldn't stop, couldn't stop—

Feet must keep on marching and feet must must be merry—

First came those dreams of marching ghosts, then wandering ghosts, see what they saw—see again, in the light as well as dark—chasing, calling—but no, couldn't stop—had to get their way to the end—

Only they never would—needed a Beginning to get to an End—

No time to look back now though—not when The End was where it always was, slunk still round the next corner—another corner that breaks its promise—looking up then round, behind, ahead—whose eyes see? Not mine, eyeless sockets implanted with eyes that aren't my own, make me see again what I have never seen before—

Same eyes as Daddy, same eyes as—

The infant-mother sees his eyes in mine, I see through hers seeing through his, see what he saw—emptied out to see, twice made alien, trapped in a time and space I'd never stepped into but can never leave—no matter where I am I'm always there, recognising everything and nothing at once—have to find something I know, know it is me who knows, listen to the waves, settle infant and mother, sound lets me come back some-how—but there is no back, born with the ghosts inside me—try though, find a point of reference, something else, something fixed, know I am seeing with my eyes, not hers, not his—

Landmarks solid enough until I come to them, dissolving soon as I approach, already have to ask the way again—and would if one figure after another wasn't swallowed up by the doors that disappeared into the disappearing houses, shops, bars— would have called out just then—asked where, did they know if—Steven where? Steven, please—if only Steven was—my throat binding my voice, the street signs erasing themselves— can only just keep on, keep going, going down some nameless, markless, endless street—

Couldn't it all just stop—just long enough to let me catch up-unmuddle what I'd heard from what I'd seen—a palimpsest of stories and silence: what my grandmother had said and my grandfather hadn't said, what speechless ghosts still make me see and what the infant-mother hid—

But out here now—see the front, hear the sea, yet dreams already slipping inside me—the seafront just there, but still—

Get myself the right side of the footlights is all I need—feel safer out of the glare—get the heels their safe spare patch of dark and watch from there—eyes my own, no catching up or keeping up—not with the dreams inside or the merry marchers out—just get myself that patch, yes—glimpsed so many through chance openings in the parade—

Lost as soon as seen—

Fleeting voids whose silent darkness flares behind the ceaseless turns of a kaleidoscope, an unfaltering servant hand labouring to placate the eye of a tyrant-child—glass pressed hard against glass, glare against glare—dazzling, delighting, blinding: the turning hand jumbles props and puppets of pantomime and parade to order, multiplied and rotated into ever-new patterns, an inexhaustible novelty that inflames the appetite it feeds. The hand, swift, ceaseless, averts the pang that waits to spit in waiting lidless eyes, the pang harboured by the pause, the pang that makes that pause a chasm, bubbling, reverberating where the circle ends, where the next begins, seeming to greet and part at once, where each glittering order is eclipsed, displaced by the next in revolutions made seamless—but there, between, where speed melts the joins, there's a flash—the promise of that safe spare patch, waiting for heels that crave the dark beneath them, that safe spare patch the right side of the footlights—

Eyes all I have to catch it—

Glimpsed and gone—

Given away and taken as pair after pair slide in and out, go back on their way, their merry marching way—

See now there—quick—a promise made by steps just left—a passage of steps that duck and dodge the hurdles as they spring and vanish, sliding, shifting—passage sliced and severed soon as it's made, redrawn and barred lest the pair that follow might try to cheat its way, steal those steps just left by a pair that found its way—way left for the taking—

Stop! Thief!

Can't take another's way, someone else's beginning, someone else's end—yes, get to The End in the end—find the ghosts, theirs to find mine—but can that be all? All that's left of their legacy? Another someone else, this Sally with her heels caught between the light that marks the dark, just watching to see how it goes, how this merry show goes on, how they do this going on still going till the going is done—going as it went with the going that's never done—waiting still for that other time where the beat stops beating, the raw heart stops bleeding, the marchers stop marching; that other time where the infant-mother sleeps, the same one where our grandmother's parents arrive, safe, and our mother's father—inspecting, collecting, is ready for the journey—going left right left to an anywhere but here, an anywhere but there, left right left to a promised land he will call home—no need to look back, that Before's been left and that After is just somewhere he lives now, where we live now—alone but together; together alone—where Steven and I go for our stroll, our paddle, share half smiles, half laughs—

Turn, let me swap places with another player—

Could take their place but not their skin—

"Oh my dear, do forgive—I thought you were ..."

My eyes come up to meet the players' eyes that have mistaken me, the apology held in their faint glimmer. Wish I were a someone else I cannot be. I see two strangers remake me into what is not there—

"Oh, unmistakeable!"

Is it my blink or theirs that breaks the spell? Sorry, my open-close mouth starts to say, says I'm not that someone else. The players' mouths mirror mine. The man bows, the woman curtsies, removing hats and half masks as they come up.

"No," the man says. "This is a friend of Mr Brody's."

It's the Scot baritone that had called after Steven earlier this evening. He draws his bowler hat through the same arc.

"The elusive Mr Brody," the woman says, taking the rose from behind her ear and handing it to me. "Any friend of Mr Brody's—"

"Oh no—I'm his sister—Sally."

"He never mentioned a sister."

"No, never mentioned—may I?" The baritone holds his hand towards me but the woman smacks it away, telling him not to bother the little thing like that.

"Mr Brody was due at nine, but as you can see ..." the baritone waves a hand the length of the woman made manikin beside him.

The doll shudders back to life. "You want us to walk you somewhere?"

"Oh no, I'm alright," I say. "I was just—"

What was I just?

The baritone's glittering mask conjures more disappointment than the player himself and whisks the woman into a twirling exit before she can volunteer them for any further services.

"You'll give our regards to Mr—"

Brody, yes—somewhere the other side of the footlights—beyond this patch, this dark; this patch, this world—this world within between worlds—this safe spare patch of dark marked out by two pools of light—gentle beacons each, sketching borders left unset and unset leaves a no-man's-land between—light that here gives up the secret treasures sprinkled in light rain, show this last step's not the last—only the last before the next—

All change!

"Spare some—"

Yes, have to keep something spare—coin to pay the ferryman, ferry you on, on to the next and no doubt need a little something too—to please your hosts and bribe the judge and put in a good word for those you leave behind—wonder if I might be able to leave the beat back there or would that have to come into the next—the next where I'd still tie double bows?—the bows, the beat—

Still beat beating on—

Beats till it—

Only it never—no, just kept on, just kept on beating, heart to the drum—

But here this world within and between where no-man's-land is everyman's, land that lies outside time between chimes—

The first of ten—

Yes! Begin!

Tick—

94

No no not yet!

Tock—

No!

Tick back, tick stop—

Oh how time—

Stops for a break by the sea—

What's the time Mr—

Don't s'pose you have the—

All the time in the—

In that other, another time, another world—can't leave this, not yet—this patch was only made for a stopover—a stop, but not the last—leave it for another, someone else, swap places with another player—I'll have their place if not their skin—my eyes change what they saw as the next player will change what I see—so move along before I'm moved along—before the beat and the rain or something prick the soles awake—nothing now, not yet, but would—fancied themselves fortune-tellers—feel the tap tap and then the beat beat—starts slow enough, slow and muffled winding up and beat beating harder faster even when there's no sign—but already: the tap without the cane, the beat without the march—no sign at all and feel that? Not a drop but still the tap, the beat, the beat beat beating through the sleeping ground—move along then and no looking back—or quick glance—

No!

Eyes off on one of their excursions, wanting to know what all the commotion under the heels was about when there's nothing—the bustle feels distant, the marchers just players, the songs drift, die out, part of the obstacle course now whittled down to strewn rubbish and stray bodies—seems the pelt and the pound are over, the parade as good as broken—there'll be nothing to match the tap, the beat—no sign ahead to explain to the eyes what the heels keep warning—

Tap—

There it is, the beat winding up while they wind up watches and wind up feet, players again marchers remasked, regrouped and ready, all picked up, keys turning in their backs: the marching way, the merry—

Oh must must be merry!

Clear the last act away and bring out the moon, coaxed out of stage fright to rise—

Higher, just a little—perfect!

Be there, yes—the tip of a shy crescent peeking over its shroud.

"Oh, I just love to walk in the rain!"

I look round but the woman standing beside me, plump and squat with a summer hat, hadn't been speaking to me—but she hadn't been speaking to anyone else either. And no, not talking to herself. No, she was sending her words out over the water.

"Never bring a brolly! Bring a brolly and it'll only stay dry and then what chance have you got?"

She seems to be asking the one boat powering its way towards the horizon, whipping a foaming white tail in its wake.

"Row row row your boat," she sings out to it. "Wonder where it goes. Where do you go, my love? Gently down the stream, merrily merrily—"

The woman walks away, singing as she goes, singing merrily merrily, her voice disappearing under the merry march clamouring to begin again, begin again yes: the fat lady might've sung but she'd still be singing, singing merrily merrily, singing, walking merrily in the rain and if not her then some other, singing on merrily in the show that always and ever goes on going on …

Slumped on a bench a player takes off his mask and gives his face a rub. Groggy eyes are prized open and, as he puts on his specs, the viewfinder widens to admit another lone player into this lone player's world. A shared nod before the eyelids droop and the smudged face falls.

"Stevie's sister," he says and takes out his cards.

Tarot. Professor Lorenzo. Or was it Lorenzino?

"Lawrence?" I ask the shuffling hands. In the mix of neon lights and street lamps I can't tell if they're the same milky eyes that had come up as Steven and I had gone into the chippie that first year, that had laboured to piece me together as Stevie's sister—*only his sister*—not *only* now: his sister. A painted clown's mouth doubles a smile. Lawrence yes—just—thankful for the flicker that muddles the face—lets me keep Lawrence as he was behind what I can't quite see now—

"You came—I remember you—you came with Stevie—to the shop, I remember—"

"That's right—is that—" I look at the still hands holding the deck.

"Tarot—yeah—read for you if you like—only—" He cut his teeth into the bloody smile, "Don't tell Stevie—you won't will you?"

Can't ask what, know I can't, but it brings back Clive's question again—

Alright is he?

The question I can't answer, the question that would have been in the hello Dad didn't give me to pass on—alright is he? Are you? My little sticky angel brother—

"'Cos you mustn't say—promise you—"

"Promise," I say and sit down as Lawrence unties the string of coloured hankies he'd pulled from his sleeve, laying the deck over them, miming a cut of the cards.

"Anyhow you like," he says, the script anchoring his voice but, just as I reach my hand, he catches it and drops it in less than the beat it takes for the painted smile to lose the double its wearer shadowed, stuffing the cards and the hankies away, clearing his throat, spilling sorrys on to the bare space on the bench between us—"Didn't mean," he starts, "didn't mean, only wanted—just for a minute—hold your hand just for a—wouldn't hurt—never hurt—ask Stevie, I never—what they said—"

"What who—" I'm stopped by the little slaps Lawrence is giving each of his hands—"badbadnaughtynaughty"—he shakes a finger over one and then holds them out towards me. He seems to want me to absolve them.

"Not true," Lawrence says, taking his hands back, patting them each better. "They made it all up—ask Stevie—he knows they made it—"

"It's alright," I say, hoping the mix of lights has pulled the same trick on my face, kept it from saying that I didn't know what was or wasn't alright, just that the hands should be forgiven. Lawrence looks up at me—or tries to—can't quite catch my eyes now though, his whole face a blink. I stretch my fingers inside the gloves.

"Hey! They're Stevie's!" Lawrence says. I'm all ready to launch into correcting him, relieved to have something I know for a fact, tell him the gloves are Clive's, but the stillness of Lawrence's face checks me—yes, the quiver across his face has settled, his hands released; seemed the chants of his accusers were silent now and his clown mouth cuts a smile that might have been his own. OK then, they were Stevie's. I put one of my gloved hands over his.

"It's really nice to see you again," I say but, soon as I do, I hear that *again* cut by the cut smile. Seeing another Lawrence now, not that Lawrence—not as he was—not that first year—seemed younger somehow, the giant humpty-dumpty all put back together but smaller—but no, it's not just that his enormous frame has shrunk, it's as though he's missing a dimension and something else—that the parts of him don't quite cohere—a chipped mosaic in the shape of a child.

"Don't tell Stevie you saw me will you? Don't tell him I was here—I did wait for him, honest I did—you can ask Martin—"

"Who's Martin?"

"Friend of ours—Stevie's and mine—keep thinking I see him—you haven't seen him have you."

"Martin?"

"Has a bowler hat always," Lawrence says.

In its absence I watch the hat draw a third arc and, hearing again Clive's voice, Steven's voice, the baritone's, see the arc return. Martin—Steven had said, yes, earlier heard him—to Clive—I'd so been tangled in how it was all not quite going, name hadn't been able to meet the face then—

"Doesn't matter," Lawrence says. "Don't like him anyway, don't want him to find me, tries to follow me—don't like him, always telling me what to do—told Stevie I don't want him round any more—always on at me, having a go, section this and section that—well he can't, they can't—I can look after

99

myself you know … won't tell Stevie will you—did wait—where'd he go?"

Somewhere in that pantomime might be—or what was left of it—show be over soon—

"Sorry, have to—" Lawrence says, getting up. "Didn't see me—don't tell—did wait—didn't see—"

Lone player joining the players; a missed counter flicked onto the board at the end of the game.

Didn't see him, no. Not Lawrence as he was who'd have known Steven as he was, a Lawrence who would mean the pattern was still in place there, waiting in case a pair might play.

The Bowler Hat. The painted clown's mouth. Another Lawrence. All part of another pattern. I look back over the railings to see a pair paddling, paddling about in the rain. Paddling about, playing out the pattern in full. The pattern. Yes, really was best as a two-hander. No other way to play it. Least not that. Another perhaps. Perhaps. Play another for now until that other time. That other when I'd be some other, some other playing at being another in that other time. Could only play what was there to play. Play out, play on—

Merrily merrily

Merrily merrily

Life is but a dream

No help in hope but still couldn't help but hope—then better start that way on—they couldn't go back—would never go back—would have to start again—start now—they'd started from nothing, with nothing, just a misspelt name, a chance letter that saved as it erased them—each of them a someone else they might have been, a someone else who knew, who went, who found The End to start again—

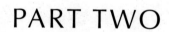

PART TWO

"Sally—are you alright?"

"Fine, yes—sorry, I shouldn't have called so late—I didn't think—"

"It's alright, it's not yet eleven, I was just getting your mother off to sleep—"

"Oh God, I didn't wake her—"

"No, no I don't think—as long as you're—and Steven—"

"Yes." I say it too quickly—

"Well, you'll say hello to him for me—"

"Of course." Of course, yes, of course I would.

"If that's all, I'd better …"

"Yes, only … I love you." It slips out like one of misshapen sorrys and I watch it sink until I hear a quick, quiet "I love you too" catch it. "You will say hello, won't you," he says.

I look at my phone for a moment after we hang up, try to shake off how odd that must have seemed—see Dad, his eyes closing, trudging up the stairs, the saucer for the pills in the morning, my mother, in and out of sleep, her gasp and swallow.

I scroll my way to Steven's number, stop, put my phone back in my pocket—

You will say hello, won't you?

Another time.

* * *

When I get back to the guest house the key won't turn and there's not much choice but to ring the bell. Clive's at the ready, his face a blotched spectrum of purplish reds, one hand gripped round a raised broom, the other lifting a torch.

"You!" Clive declares, shining the torch in my eyes. "What the bloody hell d'you think the key's for?"

"I'm sorry, yes—"

"Sorry!"

"I don't think it works—"

"There's no thinking about it. Either it works or it doesn't—and it does."

"No, but I tried it—"

"Tried it! Goes making a racket at some ungodly hour, gets me up and she says she's tried it! Give it here." Clive lowers the torch away from me to spotlight the accused. "This key", he tells me, banging the broom down, "has only just been cut. These locks only just changed so don't tell me—oh ..." Clive's eyes dip towards the key, tentative as toe in cold water. He grants me a quick look, "Bit of a mix-up it seems—yes, well never mind, just get yourself inside—and take that coat off," he says, locking up behind him, "and those shoes, I won't have you bringing that outside in." With the outside locked out and the defendant acquitted, Clive takes in a breath, recovers: "Still, there's nothing like coming out of the cold and into the warm now is there?"

"No, I suppose—"

"Nothing," Clive corrects me. "And now let's see," he says, over my shoulder as I bend to untie my laces, disabling whatever relative proficiency I've developed with the business of double bows. "Oh, never mind all that palaver," he bursts, whisking my eyes up to him, "what you want is a nice hot toddy."

"Thanks Clive, really—"

"Uncle! Uncle Clive!"

"Yes, thanks but I think I'll start heading up now."

The flaming cheeks that had just started to settle flare again. "Heading up! After all that and she says she's heading up."

Heading up. The stairs that would have to be taken, the landing that would have to be crossed. The room and the hours that wait at their end.

"Bad as that boy, she is."

Something that paired us up then, lent comfort to the scold. I hadn't felt how my face had hardened, my jaw clamped, until it released. I pull out a chair round the table we'd sat round earlier this evening, the gin bottle now standing empty between the tumblers and cards, sitting before I'm ushered into place and look up at Clive, "Thank you, that would be—"

"Lovely! Won't be a tick."

A hot toddy it is then. The nightcap. A gesture towards the pattern. A gesture before the stairs, the stairs and the landing and the room and the hours—hours waiting, hidden unhatched—wondered now at all that urgency to get back, making a fuss over the rain starting and the cold and the time, and now that I'm here, back before last orders, inside, warm, dry, that Hello of Dad's to give to Steven, but no Steven—of course no Steven, just thought, maybe—

"Hot toddies!" Clive sings, the upturned palm of a shaky hand balancing a tray of wobbling mugs. "Do things properly shall we?" I watch the tray until it has been landed safely.

"Thank you."

"Oh no no—a pleasure!"

The sound of feet thudding downstairs and the slam of a door jerks my head round, holding it there before it can turn itself back, my eyes asking Clive if it was, if it might be—wanting and not wanting the thuds and the slam to be Steven's—wanting another Steven to wander in, one I could give Dad's Hello to—

The click of Clive's tongue and double shake of his head gives me my answer.

"Oh."

"Next door, my dear," he says, sitting down with a sigh. "These walls. Paper thin."

Paper thin. Hadn't remembered that.

Unsure whether to invest his acrimony in the insensitivity of his neighbour's elephantine steps at an hour reaffirmed as ungodly, or the fact that these steps failed to be Steven's, Clive appears to have enough for both and so begins to overlap strands of mounting fury. I've always trusted Clive's monologues to be exactly that—no interlocutor required—so I only catch the snatches of speech where Clive's voice reaches the peak of his scale, privileged words leaping to cut through what had merged into a smouldering background, little more to me, unable to deter one ear from listening attentive for the door, than the sense of a tone seethe and spit, a voice race and halt.

"Sally!"

Interlocutor required. I draw the wandering ear back and return as much of myself as will comply to the body sitting present opposite Clive, sitting at the table, sitting and drinking my hot toddy, sitting and drinking and hanging on to every word.

"Yes?"

"Indeed." He pauses and lifts his chin to scratch his neck. My eyes anchor themselves on the hands holding my mug, the sound of steps getting louder, coming closer, baiting my listening ear to nip at the door. The steps stop, go on, disappear.

"Indeed, yes, my dear … but perhaps—perhaps you flatter me?"

"No, no I—"

"Well, it is the truth, I can't deny that." Clive's tone has dropped now and he leans in towards me, chewing on his lip before he goes on. "Because I am a good uncle. I am. I'm a good Uncle Clive. You know I'm a good Uncle Clive, don't you Sally?"

"Well, yes—"

"Yes?"

"Of course." I tighten my hold on my empty mug—this would be enough, this would do.

"Yes! The best! The very best! And you know," Clive says, an indulgent wink warning rather than reassuring me that all is forgiven, "you know I could be persuaded to find you a little post. Uncle Clive would put you up, see you right, see you through—yes, why you could stay in room five, room five would be yours—you would call it home—"

"That's very thoughtful and everything—"

"And I'd have Hilda train you up, teach you all she knows—"

"Hilda?"

"Ah yes! My Hilda! Hilda, all hail! You are yet to meet my Hilda? Soon remedied, she'll be serving up in the morning—seven-thirty sharp or you'll miss out—Hilda! A treat! A treasure! Her anglaise wants a bit of work but it's that sort of thing that gives the place that cosmopolitan feel—why only last week I had some fellow—let me think what was he—one of those Arab types, you know the type I mean, one of those Jews, yes, oh a proper Shylock that Arab was I don't mind saying—hence the changed locks—come to think of it, he might have been an African—because they're not all black you know—anyway my Hilda, she's from foreign parts … ask me where? Well, I can't tell you where, all I know is knowing I know—so what do you say?"

"I don't think I—"

"Well, good. You'll think about it," he says, narrowing the unpromising lull. He eyes each of our mugs in turn, presses his hands on the table and announces "Another!"

I hear something—stop it, stop it—but footsteps, I know those steps—

"You didn't like it!"

"No—no I did!"

"You didn't—you did not like my hot toddy."

"I did, really it was—"

"What? What my girl? What was my hot toddy?"

"Nice—"

"Nice!"

108

"Very nice—"

"Nice she says, nice. She, Sally, says Uncle Clive's hot toddy was … nice." Clive isn't looking at me, he's directing his words at the opposite wall.

"I'm sorry Clive—"

"Aren't they all. Sorry, yes. And a sorry bunch they'll be." Lines divide Clive's forehead into grisly rows, "Gets me up, ungodly hour—you're lucky you know, very lucky, any later and I daren't think what would have become of you, another five minutes and who knows, who can tell, who, I ask you, my dear, can say?"

"I'm really very grateful—"

"Of course you are, you're that sort, takes one to know one and all that—I think we are not dissimilar—in fact …" Clive brightens considerably at this *fact* whose full implications Clive is yet to discover—either that or he's revelling in the delay of communication. "In fact I think we are remarkably similar—remarkable!" He brings his elbows onto the table and alternates the lace of his fingers. "What I mean to say, Sally, is that we who wait, we who wonder, we who can only lay our bets … when will the little wanderer return?"

Little wanderer. Wonder if we're waiting for the same one. We. I can see Clive basking in the solace of the pronoun, eyes half closed, corners of his mouth creeping up into a smile. We. Waited, wondered, yes, but had waited and wondered then just the same, then as now, evening of that Easter Sunday he left, after the eggs, the question following me up all four flights of that house, up to the top landing, crawled up the back of my neck as I opened the window over the quiet of the street, first finding Steven in the one passer-by, then urging eyes to latch onto an old picture that saw him walking his bike along the pavement because the chain had broken, holding him there on the empty street until the sound of yapping and yelping of Mr Stern's pedigree brood returning rubbed the Little Wanderer and his bike out and there they were, six yapping, yelping spaniels pulling Mr Stern up to his front gate, up to his door, opened, closed, returning the oak-lined street to settle back into the quiet.

Little Wanderer. My ear leaning, listening. I pull it back and get up to put my coat over my arm. "Goodnight then, Clive," risking my voice just above a whisper.

"Yes, yes ... remarkable," Clive's eyes still half closed, cheeks serenely uniform, chewing on his smiling lips. "Goodnight, sweet lady, goodnight," his words taking my careful tread as far as the threshold—

"Wait!"

"Yes?" I gulp and halt at once, my guard, slumbering along with Clive, poked awake.

"I am a good uncle," he says, sitting himself up, the suddenness of his demand evaporating, a hesitant index finger trying to steady itself in the centre of his chest, "I—you do know don't you, Sally, know I'm a good Uncle Clive—you do—"

"Oh yes—"

"Yes! The very best!" and then, allowing a moment for his tone to lower itself down and find his most solemn bass, "And he knows—"

"Of course—"

"Yes, he knows I'm a good Uncle Clive—and what's more," he said, brushing the backs of his hands off, "I know that he's a good boy—not the best I grant you, but as good as good can be so I won't have you saying a word against him, you hear."

I nod, shake my head, made to wonder for a minute what I might have said—I hadn't said anything against him had I?

"Good—because it's not his fault you know—getting all mixed up with these funny doolally types, heart's in the right place—just like his Uncle Clive—just like *your* Uncle Clive ... eh, Sally." Clive had lowered head and voice together, "You don't think—you don't—" Clive wouldn't let my eyes go, they were set, gin-clear—but what? Not think what—he was asking again the question I didn't have the answer for—was he, is he—is that little sticky angel boy alright? Fine, I'd said to Dad—as if I would have said anything else, wouldn't give it too much thought would he? Not if I hadn't called only a few hours after I'd left, late enough, Brighton's Friday night bubbling around me, my mother's dreams drifting down to him ... of course I would have woken her ... Clive's waiting—Steven, fine, yes—

"Of course—" I try, willing the next words to arrive—

"Of course!" Clive doesn't need any more, he's banging an exultant fist down, his other hand clutching riches from the air. "Now go and get some rest for tomorrow, comrade, we fight on!"

"Oh Clive," I pull a glove out of each coat pocket—

Clive waves his hands at me, "No, no. You hold on to those, comrade—who knows what lies in wait, what living lark in store, who knows and who can tell?"

"Well if you're—"

"Yes, comrade—and so ... fight on!"

The general's command sends my feet to the stairs that have to be taken, takes them up to the landing that has to be crossed—I can still hear him roaring and chuckling as I turn the key, "Fight on!"

Tomorrow, yes. Battle enough. Still had the night between. Hero in the next round. Round and round. Better the battle by day, fellow battlers battling on.

* * *

Would be Lawrence's witching hour now. Witches' hour with a witch's brew. Perhaps not tonight. Can see him vanishing into the dregs of the merry band, a bowler hat bobbing over the shambling parade, milky eyes behind specs looking out for Steven.

* * *

A minute ticks over the hour. The first unhatched. Baby legs testing new life. Find the rest hiding under the sheets—

Pull them back quick, Little Miss—

Yes quick, only to find nothing—no nothing yet, no not till the dark cracks the shells open and Night has sucked the day's bones clean—then one by one out crawls each waiting hour, crawling out under closed lids and eyes that, while kept open, missed every trick, miss nothing when led by the undreamt dreams of still wandering ghosts, ghosts who find they fit just right in my skin, their bodies dug from nameless graves and burned before their bones might speak. At the window there waits the faceless face where the ghosts are taking turns and ghosts taking turns will go on taking turns until their own faces are seen, their own defaced, each made a replica of those sunken eyes and hollow cheeks that keep them indistinguishable, each face forgotten under the copy each was made to share, the copy that made each sign, the numberless numbered blended to one. Next come the faces of those that took them, last the faces that saw them taken—

Run run as fast as you can

Can't catch me I'm

No, nobody at all.

Put the side light on and the blind up and the faceless face disappears, never caught it, only my reflection—must get the window open, keep myself from being doubled. Dry out there now, see a rag doll's feet dragged along the model set. Feel like a giant up here looking down on a toy world, a toy car zooming round a bend of empty toy tracks and see now a puppet, strings just cut, he leaps, trips and the lid of a trapdoor opens to swallow his fall with only the moon to mark him—see the night so clear now, no more than wisps veiling the moon, fine and light they pass swift over her face, their race making her seem to skim read the street.

Would be down there now if a giant's jelly legs would take me, if I could work a giant's feet, if the set wouldn't break beneath them. Couldn't help seeing it all the same, the cumbersome pair kicked off and my own feet found—feet, mine yes, but not those no not, no this was a pair that went, that knew—this time yes this—yes once they were bare on pebbles just again washed clean—at least so long as I'm up here I can see it—no danger of feet seen from here mismatched by feet found on the pebbles, but from here yes—try lifting the feet though and only feel their clumsy weight against the sight of that still quiet world set upon a model set, set waiting for the next round to play, set up waiting at the water's edge.

What's that? Someone coughing. Must be Clive. Odd it should be so reassuring—no, no it wasn't Clive—was coming from outside—could be next door of course—the walls, remember, paper thin. Stopped now anyhow. Hear it still even so—coughing harder and harder and trying—who was it—trying to catch their breath now, gasping, the coughing turning to choking—someone was choking, yes sounded like someone was—horrible the way it sounds like my mother's father—

Same eyes as Daddy—ayme-eye-a-da-ee-

Coughing always coughing, gasping, choking, those Sunday visits—yes, sounded just like—

Had you that there eh, Little Miss?

Yes, very good, had me there. Keep hearing it though, hearing it in spasms but further apart now, yes getting further apart and further away. Soundtrack to that dream must be—one that caught me while it could—the coughing and the gasping and the choking coming from somewhere I could never tell where, searching and searching—get closer towards it and it starts coming from somewhere else, always the direction I've just left, room to room but never find them. Every time. Always seems as though it must have gone on and on but a look up at the clock said I couldn't have been out each time for much more than half an hour. Had never heard it like that before when I was up, unwound the sleep starting to snake its way round my ankles and up my legs, charm me away from the window I'd only just lifted a giant's hand to close, a hand shrinking to scale as it lowers the blind and screens off the toy world, left unwatched to come to life as only unwatched toy worlds can. Or so they always said. Only while you slept, they said. Trouble was that thought alone be enough to keep you up, made you sure to see a black eye wink and varnished lips purse— that was the largest of the Russian dolls, heard her tongue click too, heard the children locked inside her moan. Played dead of course soon as they were seen, or the sun came up, whichever was first. No peeking. No. All so slippery, the toy world and the dreams in rings around it, all so—dissolves at a glance, yes just as you reach, think you see—slippery as the faceless face, as sleep itself, sleep so slow to snake up, to coil round, so quick to snake off—only had to hear that coughing, that gasping, that—and it was gone. Not without a quick bite first—needs only one fang to sink a drop to trickle through the veins, make cell by cell bloat with weak weight—takes everything but the eyes—little wonder the eyes were such a useless pair of supervisors by day when they'd been scurrying and scavenging all night—behind the walls, under the floors, the chest, the cupboards, the attic, the cellar—had to find but never found—still trying to see, to catch, catch that face, the face beneath the faceless face—catch what must be seen but can't be caught, face catches the eyes, not eyes the face—same with that coughing, that gasping, that choking—can't make it out at all now that I'm listening for it—yes, have to listen out for it, need to hear it, hear where it was coming from, find it, attach it to a body, find it a face before it too slips beneath the faceless face—

Same eyes as Daddy—

Ayme-eyes-a-yoo—

How to see what must be seen, to hear what must be heard when what must will only catch, catch and not be caught, catch just as sleep begins to snake—

Then under the covers, Little Miss—

A last check of the sheets first, not that you could ever find anything with the light on and only feel something crawling either way but still—couldn't get under covers without one last—nothing—no, well of course not—

Little Miss—

Yes, yes, lights out and under the covers, wait for the rustle in the grass—no, no waiting—wait and it'll never come, look and you'll never see, listen and you'll—still couldn't help but—what was—wind had pulled the window open, rattling against the blind—where would that leave the face?—banged shut again now—wouldn't mind it open—the rattle yes but hear the sea—wanted to be down there again now—wish easy enough from here—still, just to have feet light upon the model set, set up waiting, waiting at the water's edge and there find feet bare on pebbles again and again washed clean, feet bare washed clean on pebbles washed clean, yes find feet there, feet that knew, that went—or no—no, these were feet that knew they had nowhere to go but over pebbles washed clean, feet washed clean on pebbles washed clean, feet bare on pebbles go in ankle deep—no, in deeper still, yes up to the knees, yes knee-deep: knee-deep, waist-deep—waist-deep and slide under, be drunk deep by the sea till it swallows you clean—

Just in time. Baptised on the way out if not on the way in. All the wrong way round it had to be said—and it would—my grandmother being no less capable, perhaps more capable, of offering her appraisals from her vantage point in the hereafter as she was while still prisoner of the flesh, qualifying, or rather disqualifying, the good fortune of a narrowly averted disaster in light of her revelation of what might have been—a subject on which she was a peerless authority—just in time, she'd say. Yes, just in time: drunk deep and drunk under, drunk up by the sea, drunk up and swallowed down, the whole sea drinks you up and swallows you clean—wrong way round yes and would be said yes would—but still, just in time—got there in the end she'd say yes—would she? Say that really we might have saved ourselves a lot of trouble and simply bypassed the Old Testament as she had seen fit to do—learn from her mistakes, she said, not to mention her forebears— "Oh the poor fools!"—she could only hope we'd see in the end, before it was too late, that a few drops and a priestly nod was hardly much to ask to wash the pains away ... well then, on our own heads be it—not, my grandmother was at pains to affirm—and reaffirm—that she blamed us, sinners that we were, no, she in her mercy—a mercy modelled on the All Merciful—was moved to forgive—

"Why, you weren't to know! Indeed there had been a time when even I hadn't known—oh, impossible to believe, but true—of course now that I do—just in time, thank the dear Lord, or who knows what—oh, perish the thought! It simply didn't bear—but what if I had never known? What then? Would I, like them—just been left to rot? And what of those, my own among them, in their final hour? Surely the Lord must have revealed Himself ..." His haggard majesty as it must have been then, appearing over the earthly inferno to rescue their souls, Himself redeemed in their redemption, "Yes redeemed all and all rising as One from the ash-heaped fields—oh, if only I'd known then what I know now."

Naturally she could see now what would become of them—yes she could see ... everything.

"Yes dear, everything," my grandmother would whisper to me, unburdening the terrible truth of her visions during each of the Sunday visits to see my grandfather—my grandmother and what seemed to be the same bunch of carnations having been picked up on the way—or no, not on the way but "en route!"— French being to her in her last years what English had once been—a treasured pocketful of phrases—France was where they would settle now that it was all over—"France! The Promised Land! There was family in France, his family"—and here she'd glance at the body lost under the sheets—his family were waiting in France—a conviction steeled against the passage of time, emboldened by its failure to be realised, a conviction that drew sustenance from being told and told again—it wasn't the past she replayed—once was enough—but the future, over and over, reworking it as she went—not just his family but her family too: "Indeed, had we not all met once in Vienna? Yes! I seem to recall my father-in-law distinctly, a terribly erudite man—do you know, he spoke eight languages? Eight! And you Sally will come for the holidays, n'est pas? Say oui."

This was my mother's mother of course, or, for the sake of clarification, my maternal grandmother, and perhaps she was, in her way, a way which left her wandering in the wilderness for the forty years that followed her arrival at an address in Willesden where she was to remain under the auspices of a Ms Cox—or, as my grandmother later concluded, a lady going by the name of Ms Cox—who would provide bed and board for the poor dear in return for domestic and administrative assistance until her parents and brothers (sometimes an elder sister or a cousin was included here) came to relieve said Ms Cox. In the mean time this Ms Cox would, as far as was possible, school her charge in the elocution proper to her nation, the manners proper to her household and, most importantly, "make sure you was keep busy as thumb twiddling only leads to tears". Of course the girl was most welcome, of course, there was no question she'd take her in, it was the right thing, the Christian thing to do—you heard such dreadful stories—there was only one condition—Ms Cox was nothing if not fair— which she was quite sure would be understood:

"Not a word breathed inside or out about the (ahem) journey and keep that voice down until that (ahem) accent wears off a bit. Hush hush, yes dear? And before I end up getting funny looks from next door, no more of that wailing in the night—oh yes my lamb, I know, but there's nothing I haven't seen come out in the wash and what good did wailing ever do anyone? Certainly never got supper on the table and I've got some (ahem) suet over so we'll have pudding tonight—what do you say to that? Pudding? Come now or you'll ruin that face of yours and I'll have to show you how to make it up all over again—oh dear, what'll I do with you? They'll be along before you can say Jack Robinson"—Ms Cox was quite sure about that—"but you know what happens to watched pots."

Unfortunately my grandmother did not—not then—but she would learn—Ms Cox would see to that—not that she'd need to as it turned out—no, Ms Cox might have been wise—wise as she was fair—but not as wise as her newly arrived Austrian charge would soon be and a quick brush of the dust off that last sight of her mother and brothers stepping out onto the street in the Vienna she'd left just two weeks before told her in no uncertain terms that watched or not that pot would never boil.

"Forty years I wandered," she'd tell me, "forty years in the wilderness"—a span which allowed her to improve upon each of her reinvented selves: ancestry, place of birth, mother tongue, name—all edging their way from Vienna to London until Clara Weiss was Claire White, firstborn to Mr and Mrs Christopher White of Dollis Hill, educated at Willesden grammar, minded her t's and u's, the first to wave her flag for Rule Britannia and despair at the sudden influx of all sorts—

"What a dreadful hotchpotch it is these days, nothing like I remember, well it can't go on unless we wanted to all be crammed together like sardines, there just simply isn't room"— scrubbing away as best she could all traces of the girl who'd been sent and the alien who'd arrived, the God she'd grown up with, already fragile as the merry band marched and the train doors closed, disintegrating utterly by the time she was on the platform at Liverpuddle Street, thumb holding the little brown leather notebook open where her mother had written the address, trying to show someone, to stop them, to ask, the girl who knocked at number thirty-four where there was no Ms Cox—

"Oh, Ms Cox—she's the green door with the pansies—"

The girl who, on a day in June that didn't look anything like a June she'd ever seen before, was (ahem) welcomed, who waited and learned not to wait. Wise, very wise, yes—

119

"Yet the Truth was still to be revealed and without the Truth in the wilderness would I wander—but what would keep and sustaineth?"

I can picture the girl my grandmother painted of herself—small featured, slight, and powdered just right as Ms Cox taught—but not the Sally who sat at her grandmother's feet, sitting on the floor of the room her grandfather had been put in, Steven sent to go and play before that fidgeting drove everyone mad or he broke something or—our parents outside whispering with the nurse and the doctor as they always did for the best part of the visit and so I would be sitting there, my grandmother's hush hush voice as trained by Ms Cox coursing over the tight arrhythmic breaths coming from the body threatening to twitch awake. That talk, the "wandering", the "wilderness"—the confessionals came weekly but even so, even now, I can't say I really ever grasped what kept and sustaineth. But my grandmother—my wiser than Ms Cox grandmother—was no fool!

"No, no, no!"

No, she, in her wiser-than-Ms-Cox-wisdom, had taken out ample spiritual insurance:

"Kosher on Shabbat and a seat in the back row of a nice C of E on the Day of Rest."

She had considered other variations on the theme of Christ but it was on account of the British that she'd been saved in this world and there was little doubt that if any God would see to her salvation in the next it would be their's—

"Theirs? Am I not Clara White of Dollis Hill? I might have married a Baum—"

"A Baum?" The announcement was too much for even Ms Cox to maintain the hush hush voice she herself championed.

"Yes, Ms Cox, a Baum."

But she was not Baum by blood, she was White! She was Clara White of Dollis Hill! "Dollis Hill through and through!"

Well, that settled that, Anglican it was, well, it was Anglican on a Sunday, her Saturday God, pestering her with his talk of the first commandment, hadn't died quite so easily as she'd thought, resurrected every Friday with all that "to-do" her husband went in for—

"How he can just sit there with that nasty number under his sleeve and thank the same God who'd let both our families be fed to the ovens for the wine and the bread I'll never know—"

The worst of it the candles that lit up more than twenty years of Friday night blessings round the kitchen table in Vienna. She didn't like to complain, she wasn't one to complain— particularly when there was no one to complain to—a shiver of a glance towards the body under the sheets was sometimes inserted here—but, try though she did, it wasn't long before she had to concede what was ruthlessly apparent: appeasing the demands of two jealous Gods was more than she could manage and so, until the Truth came to tidy it all up, she had to weigh up the pros and cons and in the end came to the inescapable conclusion that all things being considerably less than equal it was a Christian God who took better care of his children: "If it wasn't for the twist of fate that costumed me with blonde hair and blue eyes who knows what would have happened?" Well she did. She knew precisely what: "I'd have been stamped with a number just like my darling Bernie—just as well I'd seen to that nasty number or who knew what might— better to keep your head down, not look left, not look right, and make a frightfully good show of sending off the carol singers to raise money for the lifeboats."

Her wanderings would have overstepped their forty year due had "that lovely girl Carmel not shown up—just in time too Sally, or who knows what?—to sort out that terrible mess your grandfather had gone and made of his arm—"

"But he—"

"Now now dear, just a little accident, hmm …"

"Just a little—"

"Very good, dear, very good—where was I? Carmel, yes, lovely Carmel—oh Sally," she'd say to me, "you would have liked Carmel very much, oh how you would have liked her for a sister, yes Sally dear, she'd be a lovely sister for you. Well now, this Carmel—lovely—yes I did say—very efficient, wasted no time at all putting me in the know, yes this Carmel told me right away what was what—even held off finishing up your grandfather's dressing till she'd taken me through it all. Mrs Baum, she said—Madame Blanche! I said, but you must call me Claire."

So Carmel, calling my grandmother Claire—"I insist!"—laid Mrs Baum's nee Weiss, husband's undressed arm back on his lap—"It could wait," Carmel had said, there were more important matters, "matters that cried out for attention—could she not hear?"

"Hear what, dear?"

And here Carmel, "lovely Carmel!", took Madame Claire Blanc's hand—"this hand Sally dear, she took this hand"— between her own two lovely hands and said she could see—"What, dear, what?"—

"Everything."

Now Ms Cox might have been wise, Ms Cox might have been very wise, Miss Claire White—or Madame Blanche or

Blanc—might have owed Ms Cox the foundation upon which she had built and tended her own wisdom that had kept and sustaineth—a wisdom melting away between lovely Carmel's lovely hands—but however wise Ms Cox might have seemed to the impressionable (ahem) Clara Weiss, Ms Cox could not see, not as Carmel could see, not as she herself, as Madame Blanche nee White would see—"thank heaven for heaven-sent Carmel"—everything.

Yes, Carmel could see a woman in need—

"You can?"

"Great, great need," and Carmel could see the road that had been laid down ahead: "A road that descended, descended, down, down, to the very pit of—"

"Stop!"

She could see—"and not just for you Mrs Baum—"

"Blair Clonk!"—

"But for your husband, your children, your children's children ..."—

"That's you, Sally dear," my grandmother told me, reaching for my hand which quickly obliged—

"Your children's children's children's—but there is, if you are willing—"

"Yes?"

"If you want, truly want—"

"Truly!"

"To be saved, redeemed—"

"Redeemed? Whatever for?"

Carmel shook her lovely head, took a lovely index and rested it ever so gently beneath an eye—"Everything Mrs Baum."

"Everything?"

"Everything."

"Oh, I had feared as much, of course it was only a matter of time, I will be found out at the last, they will come for me—but they can't, look, my own arm—look!—Is there a number? No—you see, I am good, pure, I'm not some dirty—it's only Bernard—my Bernie—and I've seen to that—"

"Precisely," Carmel had said. "*Pree*-cisely."

"But they won't come for me—my skin, milk white as any Aryan's and oh—too terrible it was, Sally, too, too—but I *am* a good person—"

"Really?" Carmel didn't think it was wise to assume as much just yet.

"I am!"

Well, Carmel was only too sure Mrs Baum—

"Madame—oh, but what is the use?"

"None Mrs Baum. None at all." Yet Carmel was sure Mrs Baum meant to be a good person but … "Let's see, have you never stolen?"

"Never!"

"Ever told a lie?"

"Never!"

"Not even a little tiny white lie?"

"Never!"

"Madame Blanche?"

My grandmother's eyes had the flames of censorial bonfires in them, burning the words as she spoke: "Not a word of this, Sally," she said, "but she could see and there was no use in—none at all—but still! There was a way—and there is—for you too, for us all—they're coming for us—marching through the streets they come—"

The merry band marching flying the merry flag of fun!

"Twice licked to a cinder by the devil's own tongue—but for Carmel. Lovely, lovely Carmel. Carmel who saw, who'd been sent—heaven sent!—Lovely Carmel, with the spirit of the Lord within her declared us for Jesus here on earth—darling Sally, Carmel explained it all: the messiah has come!"

She stopped, passed a hand over her hair, closed her eyes. My grandmother had this way of turning her faintly smiling face upward that would make a velvet hush settle over the room and you could almost see it being draped over the body under the sheets, covering its conspicuous invisibility, its strained breath, a blanket of untouched and untouchable snow denying the dips, the ridges, the tracks made beneath. The shroud of silence seemed frozen as I watched my grandmother's lips mouth those revelatory words puff thick and quick as breath in cold air—only then there had been sirens, the softly closed eyes had sprung open and each hand, made a claw, gripped the seat of her chair, her lips twitching and pursing, twitching and opening—my eyes, running along the carpet, had found a stain and locked to it—if the siren would just stop, move away—but instead a second joined it and my grandmother screamed to make a trio and under it all my grandfather's breath, growing tighter and tighter, gasping, coughing, coughing turning to choking. They'd all rushed in then—my mother, Dad, the nurse—or no, it was my mother, she'd rushed in, gone straight to the bedside, Dad behind, looking at me, asking what was the matter and the nurse sucking in her cheeks as she took

125

out the file from the end of the bed and clicked her pen. The sirens had stopped, the screaming had stopped, the gasping, the coughing—all stopped—only the nurse's pen scratching its unhurried way over the page, and my mother's voice at the bedside, "It's OK," she kept saying, stroking her father's head, "it's OK"—the sirens, the screaming, the gasping, the coughing, the coughing turning to—yes, sounded like he was—"OK, it's OK"—all stopped. The file was closed, put back and the nurse clicked her pen shut. Her chin doubled as she tucked it into her neck to see better the watch pinned at her breast—"It's coming on for dinner time," she said, and they didn't allow visitors while they were doing the dinners—

"But we always stay with him while he has his—"

"Well, that's against the rules, strictly speaking and we can't go on making exceptions—in any case, we've just been getting Mr Baum into a nice routine, he'd had all his soup yesterday, yes you did, didn't you, Mr Baum? Yes, and then after dinner we'll have a look at that arm of yours, healing up nicely."

At that my grandmother's face screwed itself into a maze of livid veins: "You leave his arm alone," she hissed, "you leave him—don't you touch his arm."

The nurse looked at her watch again. "I'll be back shortly," she said and said something again about how it wasn't right and the doctor wouldn't be happy and how she'd explain this business she didn't know and—

Dad had put his hand on my grandmother's shoulder, and I can see it now, never forget that, maybe because it was the one time I'd seen him do that and she hadn't flinched—or spat—"One of them," she'd always told me—

"Let's take you home now, Clara," Dad had said and she'd asked how he could when they were outside waiting for her

126

and he said she was quite safe so long as she didn't look left or right—"Just look straight ahead, Clara," he'd said—"yes, that's it, straight ahead"—and she let herself be helped up and her arm linked and kept repeating to herself as they went, "Straight ahead, straight ahead" and, overlapping my grandmother's repetitions, Dad's "That's right, that's right," and behind them my mother at the bedside repeating, repeating, "It's OK, it's OK," and under them all the breathing, not gasping or coughing, just breathing, but tight, so tight and that tight breathing all that was there, all that was left now that my mother was silent and my grandmother gone and Dad gone and the nurse gone—but she'd be back and they'd start all the fuss with the soup, bringing the spoon up and the face turning away, pressing into the pillow and the nurse with her "Come on now Mr Baum" and my mother saying "Please Daddy, please," and odd it always felt when she said that—"Daddy"—and me wanting to take the spoon out of the nurse's hands because every time it came close to my grandfather's mouth the coughing started again, nurse pressing the spoon to his lips and then him coughing again—but Dad couldn't be long—better I found Steven now so we'd be all ready and there wouldn't be all that waiting, just get in the car and be home—

I'd found Steven in the little garden by the car park, sitting on the grass, pulling up handfuls of it—"Is it time to go?" he'd asked when he saw me and I'd answered by asking what he was doing and he'd said nothing so I just sat down next to him and we didn't say anything really, just sat there, both of us just pulling up handfuls of grass.

It was always quiet in the car till we reached the Hendon Way. "You should have told the nurse to give him something," my mother would say then, or "Why didn't you tell the nurse?"—or else something about the doctor—"I didn't like the doctor, Daddy doesn't like the doctor, I can tell, or the nurse—he hated the nurse—"

"How can you be so sure?" Dad would ask—

"Because I am—because he's my father, that's why."

And then it would all be quiet again except on that one Sunday my mother was saying it all the way back, how she just knew, and she supposed it must be all her fault—"Well it's not my fault, I always said Daddy should come and stay with us, if he'd come to stay with us none of this would ever have happened."

Just in—

Not this time—

Or who knows what might—

Nothing dear, nothing—

Nothing?

Nothing—

No, nothing might never—

No, might not—

No, nothing might never happen—only it already had. I knew—Steven too—he'd been there—both of us had seen it—seen our grandmother, our grandfather's arm, seen her take it and the cigarette in her hand and the cigarette burning in quick light jabs to scar the number that had scarred Bernard—"My Bernie! Scarred! Condemned! Meant for the ovens!"—delete the number that deleted him—

"But it was just a little accident," our grandmother was explaining, "a little accident is all and a little accident is no one's fault now is it?"

Dad said it didn't look so little to him and it would have to be seen to—

128

"No," our grandmother said, "that won't be necessary, I've seen to it myself," and she pointed towards the browned, damp bandages our grandfather had tugged off—"Too hot," he had been saying, "too hot, too tight."

That morning was a couple of weeks before the Sunday afternoon visits would begin, before that same bunch of carnations was first bought and my grandfather was still more than that body lost under sheets, retrieved only for the sake of note-taking and soup—he was sitting at the side table taking out the contents of his pockets, holding up each of his gathered miscellany for examination. Steven had said he wanted to have a look and went and sat by him, mimicking the process of taking up whatever had just been inspected, placing it right in front of an eye and then holding it up to the light. My mother came in from the kitchen then, saying they couldn't, they just couldn't, but before she could say what they just couldn't she told Steven he really shouldn't be bothering his grandfather like that—

"But what's all this?" my mother asked her father "Where did you get all this, Daddy? Daddy?"

He waved her voice away and began busily shaking his head at a wrapper which, it seemed, had not passed the test. He handed it to Steven and took a gulp of air, coughed it back up and spat into the shredded tissue he'd left in his pocket.

"It's worse," my mother was saying, "it's definitely worse, don't you think it sounds?"—and she looked over at Dad who was picking up his coat and my grandfather's coat and saying he'd take him now—"Well, get them to listen to his chest while you're there," my mother said, "I don't like the sound of it."

"Nothing wrong, nothing to fear, all fine fine fine," my grandmother chanting before soothing her own neglected chest with a pat and saying how she'd said he'd catch cold out and to take a scarf and not to be so long and it was asking fate to have her nasty way with him—

"Out—when was he?—why didn't you?—oh Daddy, you promised you—"

"It's alright, dear, he always comes back, nothing wrong, nothing to fear, all—"

"Yes, take him now," my mother said, "and don't forget his chest because it really is sounding much much—"

"No one taking my Bernie anywhere," my grandmother said, lurching up.

"Just have this arm of his seen to—" Dad started.

"Silly billy," my grandmother said, "silly billy Baum—just a little accident, just had a little—"

"See to his arm and they can listen to his chest and—"

"No," my grandmother said, "you never know what those doctor types get up to—"

"It's alright," Dad said. "I'll be there. I'll make sure everything is OK—"

"How dare you! It is I—his wife!—who makes sure every-thing is—" she stopped, the prance of her spittle-flecked words arrested. She was going to comb her hair, "Yes," she said, "I will comb my hair now, I have always had lovely, lovely hair."

My mother went and knelt down at her father's side, "You'll let them make you better won't you, Daddy? They can see to your chest and your—" her father's head again busily shaking redirected her—"What's all this for?" she asked, placing her hand over his—he had turned to her then, his head still,

"For the journey," he said, and at that Steven said he wanted to come—

"Can't I? Please!—and Sally too—and the cat—when Michael goes on holiday they always take the—"

"Who's Michael?"

"No!" Our grandmother couldn't believe her ears she said. "Take the cat? Cats are horrible creatures!"

Dad gave Steven the look that told him he'd better be quiet or—

"The journey?" our mother asked—

"Shush and hush and leave him alone now, dear," our grandmother scolded, putting her comb back into her purse, "hush and shush and—"

Our mother, still with her hand over his, asked where he was going and our grandmother announced that no one was going anywhere—"anywhere at all!"

Our grandfather put down the penny he'd been holding and looked up at our mother. "Got to get ready," he said, and she said they were going to see to his arm first, "It looks very sore, is it very sore? They'll see to your arm, Daddy, and have a listen to your chest—it sounds worse, does it feel—because it sounds and his arm—it looks—" but he took his hand back from under hers and picked up the penny—

"Little accident is all, just a little—"

"Please now, Clara—"

"Little—just a little—"

"Daddy what—"

Our grandfather dug into each of his pockets, found a scrap of tissue and began rubbing the penny with it—

"Your arm, what—?"

I just kept looking at my toes pointing up in my shoes—wouldn't look up, not let my mother see my face—because she'd be able to tell—she'd know—and not look at Steven and not—but Steven was looking at our grandfather blowing on the penny and rubbing it, blowing and rubbing before he said "Little accident, little accident is all and a little accident is no one's—"

"No one's fault at all!" rang our grandmother's voice, finishing the words she'd taught so well, a bright slice through the mutter still repeating: "Little accident, little accident is all and a little accident is no one's—"

"What little—Daddy, what little?"

Our grandfather's face shaded into a smile as he looked at his daughter, looking at her as though from a distance so that it seemed for a moment that it was our mother, not our grandfather, who was incomprehensibly far away. Our grandfather's smile didn't slip as he spoke, "Someone must have stubbed their cigarette out, yes must have stubbed—little accident," he took the penny out of the tissue then and handed it to Steven, "Look at that," he said, "good as new."

"Good as new," Steven said, smile so wide it seemed to reach out beyond his face.

"Lucky," our grandfather said, "it's a lucky penny."

"Can you prove it?" Steven asked, smile shrinking.

Our grandfather shook his head: "Find a penny, pick it up …" and Steven finished the rhyme with him. "See," our grandfather said, "lucky," and put the coin into the centre of Steven's palm and closed his hand around it.

Once Dad and our grandfather both had their coats buttoned up and were at the door our mother started about his scarf:

"Are you sure you'll be alright like that—wouldn't you like to take your scarf, really you should—he shouldn't be out without it," she said to my father, "not with his chest as it is—no, I really don't like the sound of his chest, it's worse, I'm sure it's—Daddy does it feel any …?"

But he was back at the side table, putting his collection back in his pockets, bursting an "Oh for God's sake!" out of Dad and an "Oh Daddy!" out of our mother. Steven announced he was going too; he wanted to come he kept saying until I elbowed him in the ribs—"Just 'cause you don't want to go," he said—and he was right, I didn't want to go, but I didn't much want to be sitting there either—"Can't we?"—I began but our grandfather was putting his collection back, mouthing a count of his goods and Steven said not to worry, he'd keep watch, a promise which rewarded him with a nod, a promise he kept with great nobility, taking up the chair our grandfather had sat at and replaying the process as observed: each item up to the eye and then up to the light, save the moments his scabbed knee was too much to resist while I, for my part, picked at the embroidered cushion, eyes up each time my mother took the steps to the door and back …

"It shouldn't be taking so long, what could be taking so long—I should have gone with them, I knew should have gone, how could I have let them go without me, I should never—there must be something wrong and how could your father not at least call, he should call, just say it was alright—something must—yes I'm sure something's wrong—they must have had an accident—"

"Little accident dear," began our grandmother—

"Oh, what if something's happened—"

"Nothing dear, nothing."

"I'll never forgive myself—"

"But a little accident is no one's fault," and later on Dad would report that our grandfather had parroted the same: "Little accident," he'd told the doctor who'd said it didn't look so little to him—

"But did they listen to his chest?" my mother demanded.

"Yes, they listened and it's fine but the burn's infected and the dressing will need to be changed—someone will have to come round—"

"Someone!"

"A nurse, yes a nurse would be sent round—the doctor's concerned—"

"The doctor's concerned!"

"As I said myself, it's time to start thinking about organising some proper care."

"Oh is it now? You must be very pleased with yourself—I suppose you told the doctor what a terrible daughter I am—"

"No one's fault, dear," my grandmother corrected—

"And what else did he say?" my mother asked. "Why didn't you just go and say what a dreadful mother I am too?"

"Now you're just being—"

"Being what?"

"This isn't the time," Dad said and then turning to our grandmother, "A nurse will be coming—"

"I am not having a nurse here!"

"Yes you are, Clara. Now I think it's time we all said goodbye."

Our mother had sat down then and pressed rigid fingers over her head, saying they couldn't, they just couldn't, but what they just couldn't she never said and went over to her father who was sitting back in his chair. "We're going now," she told him and kissed him on the forehead.

"Not going," he said, taking her hand.

"Yes," she said, "going—but we'll be back soon, be back tomorrow—"

"Going," he said, "where are you going?"

"Going home," she said.

"Home, home," our grandfather echoed.

"Yes, that's right."

"Home," he said moving his hand over his valuables, "I was on my way home too."

* * *

At the window there waits the faceless face for the last ghost to take his turn, a turn he has taken and will go on taking until his own face is seen, the face of a man as his ghost wears his face, his face before his face was made a copy, defaced to make a sign, the face of another listed and numbered, another whose number replaced his name, this man, just another, displaced left to wander, his ghost still trying to find his way home.

* * *

So put the light on and the blind—no, leave it down, world below doesn't want watching, outside eyes, sent its players scrambling for the dark, made them wait till they could begin the scene again, let them play it out then—it's the turn of the toy soldiers now, they know not to keep them from their left, right left: left right left, left right left—stopping every few paces to knock on the ground—

"Open up! Open up!" says Number One.

"What?"—that's Number Two—

"Nobody home?" is scripted for the privilege of Number Three.

"Well then," says Number Four, whose honour it is to start them up again: left right left, left right—

"Hmm … knockety knock!"—all four this time—"We know you're in there! Nobody? Open up!"

Now, our toy soldiers have been made just like other toy soldiers except for a singular oversized feature bestowed upon each that denotes their gift and role: Number One's is an eye, his left, a magnificent bulging orb, perfectly round and three times larger than any ordinary eye, Number two has a nostril, his left, six times the size of Number One's eye, a magnificent cavern and it is this very nostril that has been set twitching—a twitch that directs the next left right left—ah yes, but it is the third whose ear has been blessed—his left, magnificent, nine times the size of Number One's eye, it pricks and directs the next left right left until the fourth unrolls his tongue, most magnificent of all, thrice nine times the size of any ordinary tongue, thrice nine times in thickness and thrice nine times in length, he stops, considers, tastes the air—corporeal fluids (fermenting), flesh-eating-flesh (rotting) of—apologies, he must excuse himself …"Sincerest," he says, bile rising, glands pinching, a hot wave—"Must dash" and, oops-a-daisy, he vomits into the pit.

Number One laughs, "This must be the spot! Knockety knock!"

Number Four, recovering, joins the rest (though he wouldn't mind a lie-down). Together they circle the trap door and stamp their arrival. Of course it's Number One who pulls the door open to spy with his magnificent eye—

"Nothing!"

Nothing?

"Oh ho ho, we'll see about that," and down reach a flurry of hands: they fish, they flap, they fumble—

"See? Nothing!"

"Call this nothing?" says Number Two, pulling up the swallowed puppet.

"What", ask Numbers Three and Four, the rag doll between them, "do you call this? How'd she end up down there?" They turn each upside down and give them a good shake—nothing out of the doll, grubby odds and ends out of the puppet—

"Puppet! What good's a puppet without any strings? There must be something else on them—" they strip them and dig into orifices between stitches and hinges, yank off her plaits, twist his limbs—

"Nothing!"

"Nothing?"

"Not a thing!"

Number One blames Number Two and Number two blames Number Three and Number Four sticks out his tiny tongue and says "It's not fair there's no Number Five," and kicks the "silly stupid doll and the silly stupid puppet" back down the trap door—only too happy to oblige, greedily snapping up its regurgitated feed—"Silly stupid, not even a puppet, how can you even call that a puppet when it hasn't got any strings?" But numbers One to Three are already left right lefting off—

"Hey! Wait for—"

All gone and Number Four is huffing, puffing, shuffling after …

Safe to creak open the lid now, let eyes peek out and hands appear, but not until there is only the sound of the sea do the doll and puppet clamber out. The doll sits herself up, adjusts her head—it keeps lolling onto her shoulder—takes the torn-off plaits to drape over her bald head—"My hair! I have always had such lovely hair!"—she rubs one eye and runs her fingers along a broken seam while the puppet untangles his legs, touches the joints where the strings were cut, the scraped limbs—all chipped but at least wood cannot bruise. He crawls about to gather his scattered belongings—where was the button? There had been another wrapper and the tissue—"Aw, easy does it"—up he'd have to get—"Where are you off to now?" the doll asks—

"Collecting," he says, "be back."

The rag doll watches him as he goes, "Yes yes, nothing to fear, always comes back, little puppet always comes back. My little Bernie always …" He picks up what he can, filling his pockets, they will be full again soon and soon he'll be ready for the journey and soon he will be home.

* * *

"But you are home," our mother had said.

Our grandfather's head started its busy shaking again. "If you bury me here," he said, "I'll never get back."

* * *

Blind left down then, wasn't right to put it up when that world set up below was doing its best to keep on turning on the set, its toy players their best to play it out at last, couldn't always be making them stop and start, over and over and night after night, the same scene always and having to start from the beginning—never did let them get to the end before the light arrived, consuming them ever so quietly with a cool white flame and, above them each time, the clouds having to thicken and gather, doing what they could to sop up the end of a dawn still bleeding into the sky. Let them play it out then— had never got to the end and so had to keep on—had to when once was enough—yes, our grandmother had said that—once was enough, she'd said, yes—so no more of this up and down with the blind, it was down so leave it down till it could come up safely on to players that were meant to be seen—as it was then, good—but the light? Could keep that on, yes, just while I get a splash of cold water at the sink—stops you feeling sick— yes, that's better—

And now under the covers—

Yes, under the covers. Such careful steps across the room—here they were, those light feet, so delicate when no delicacy was needed, as though there were a sleeping body below to wake— take more than clumsy steps to wake Steven even if he had come back—once he was out he was out—and he was out soon as his head hit the pillow, or so he always said—only, remember that night with our mother and the pills, not long after her father had died and Dad saying our mother wasn't well and she'd be going away for a little while—

"Why?"

"So she can get better."

—and Steven asking all day if she was going to die because she was always saying she was going to die and maybe now she really was and let him sleep in my room, his was too hot or too cold or—

"Sally?"

"Yes."

"Are you asleep?"

"Yes. Are you?"

"Yes."

"Sally, is mum going to die?"

Soon as his head hit the pillow. So our mother went away to a place to make her better that couldn't make her better—

Was Steven already back at the guest house? Sure he hadn't come back, would have heard, of course after all that he could've slipped in—no, he never slipped in—if he came back he came back—still, might have drifted off and just not heard—had I drifted off? Couldn't tell sometimes. Feet kept themselves quiet anyway, or habit kept them quiet—habit that had never been anything but lost whether he was there or not— his room below mine in that house too—my room on the top floor, Steven right below and our parents' beneath his—always seemed to be this unbroken weave of dreams laying a blanket between me and the beat.

* * *

The bar had been dressed for breakfast, or rather three of its tables had been. Clive's sitting at one, giving morose consideration to a butter knife. "It's not right," he's saying as I come in. My entrance is another cause for disappointment: "Oh," he says. "I thought you were—never mind, sit down."

Glancing between the two empty tables does little to improve the situation. "No no!" Clive cries, patting the seat of the chair next to him. "At the captain's table!"

"Right, thanks," I say, eyes on the patted seat. A quick rummage and I find an adequate smile, edging my way towards the designated spot. Clive looks up at the clock. "You're late!"

"But you said—"

An insistently cheerful elbow jabs the air in my direction, darting my hand back from the chair. Without getting up, Clive lurches his arms over and pushes it back, scraping its legs along, "There," he says with a wheeze, "sit!" The imperative drops me into the chair and crosses my legs to lock me in place. "Only joking!" Clive laughs himself into a wheeze. "Late? You? Never! Hah! Oh it's only your old Uncle Clive having a joke with you—you don't mind a little joke now do you, Sally?"

"No of course—"

"Of course not! Now there's a good girl—you could teach that boy a thing or two about punctuality. Naturally I'm here from seven to meet and greet," he nods at the empty tables before turning back to me. "What'll you have?" He puts his hand up, "No, hang on, hang on," reaches for the knife and spoon laid at my place, checks them over. "Alright," he says, smacking them back in front of me, "what's it to be?" I haven't quite hesitated before he lunges again, "Christ almighty, girl, take all day about it and it won't be breakfast—we've gone all Continental this morning—Hilda!—cooker's playing up—petit pain?" The basket of rolls is swung up to advertise.

"Thank you."

"You might but I doubt the rest of my customers would be quite so forgiving—imagine my having to explain the absence of eggs and bacon to a full house of expectant guests—lot of

animals they can be this time of the day with empty bellies—
Hilda! Where is she?" A bang on the table shudders the
inspected cutlery, plates, and bowls with it. My stomach threat-
ens to creep up towards my throat but I'm released from the
effort to make a reply as Clive gets up and goes to the bottom
of the stairs, "Hilda!" The third call brings feet rushing down.
Something drops and a pleading "Ah no!" ejects Clive from
his chair.

"What on—" Clive rescues the cup that had bounced at his
feet, a darting squirrel of a woman appearing just after. I think
it's safe to assume this is Hilda. She grabs the cup out of his
hands and tucks it into the basket in her arms.

"What the hell are you doing, girl?" he demands as Hilda
scurries towards the kitchen.

"Bed change," she clips as she goes.

"Stop! No no—no bed change—breakfast—excuse me, Sally."

Rising voices clash and compete, crockery drops into the sink.
Hilda scurries back in, her pink face glistening, eyes blinking,
"Bed change, bed change."

Clive's right behind her, "Breakfast, breakfast, this time breakfast time, later time bed change time," his commands' increasing volume forfeiting sense. Hilda tosses all efforts at English
aside, explaining herself in her native tongue.

"Enough! Enough!" Clive's hands flap, Hilda's follow, four
hands mimicking the furious confusion of voices, flapping
themselves into a blur. My stomach inches up again, closing
my eyes. I swallow, steadying eyes on the far corner of the window frame—alright, it's alright—stomach inching back now
but my throat closes, instructing the eyes to keep themselves
where they were. Obedience is rewarded: by the time my
eyes approach the scene again the flapping hands have been

subdued, each released back to their owners who wear them with caution—one of Clive's attending to various itches on the back of his neck, the other put away in his pocket while both of Hilda's occupy themselves with the tears streaking a muddle of trails down her pink cheeks.

"Look," Clive says, his eyes just past Hilda, moving in half steps towards her and, though he isn't quite close enough to reach her, urges a reluctant hand to pat her shoulder. With his arm still outstretched, the hand having been suspended mid-air finding itself rather more eager to pat, Clive takes the necessary remainder of half steps, eliciting a squeal from Hilda before the hand that felt it really must pat could pat. Hilda, unpatted, jerks away and flounces in the direction of the kitchen, avenging herself by way of cupboards opened and slammed, utensils clattered and dropped. Clive throws the offending hand up. "What? What did I do?" I blink the answer I don't have and settle my eyes back on the far corner of the window. "I don't know, I don't know," Clive sighs, sitting back down to make a slow-motion lunge for another roll, giving it an unconvinced stab with his knife—he halts—turning his knife towards the untouched roll in front of me, insisting I bring my eyes straight to the table—manners!

"My breakfast not good enough for you, eh?"

Slow, certain steps making their way down magnetise Clive's gaze towards the bottom of the stairs. "Well well well," he says, getting up, aligning another "well" for each of his strides to Steven. "If it isn't Little Lord Fauntleroy."

"Morning Clive, Sal." Steven pulls out the last chair at the captain's table.

"Allow me," Clive says with a bow, shaking out a serviette, letting it float on to Steven's lap only to have to watch the serviette being removed and put back on the table.

"A roll for sir," Clive sweeps up the basket, lifting up a roll into the air before dropping it. The scene slows down as the roll bounces off a side plate and on to the floor.

"Nice one, Clive," Steven says, leaning back.

"Sir really should be more careful."

"Is there a paper around here somewhere?"

"Yesterday's", a deflated Clive answers sitting back down, "on the counter … Oh no you don't!" Steven taking up a stool and the paper is sufficient to cause Clive's alarm. "You're in company! Get that behind of yours back here—and give me that paper—my paper! And eat your bloody breakfast—"

"Doesn't look much like—"

"It's Continental—Sally hasn't complained—Sally likes my Continental breakfast—Sally—"

"Alright Clive, alright—"

"Is it? Is it?"

Steven and Clive match raised brows and silent chewing. Clive's turn to lean back now. "So," he says, "good night was it—didn't hear you come in. Mrs Sergeant was it?"

"No, Clive—"

"A lady then?"

"No, Clive, not a lady—"

"A whore? Don't tell me—"

"No—Clive, would you just—"

"Not a whore?"

"No."

"A bore!"

"No, Clive."

"I give up—let's see if Sally can get it. Sally—no! No, hang on ... not a whore, not a bore—I've got it! It's that ponce with the bowler hat!"

"Martin's not a ponce."

"You're a rent boy!"

"Yes, Clive, I'm a rent boy."

"You never!" Clive's voice as explosive as his face: eyes bulging, cheeks bursting, "You!"

Steven shakes his head with the disinterest of a door left to close itself and picks the paper back up.

"Well, just don't you forget," Clive says, "that's my paper." He turns to me, "And now, how should our most distinguished guest like to be entertained this fine morn?"

"Me—I don't think I—"

"Give me that," he snaps, snatching the paper off Steven. "Thank you. I apologise my dear, I've polished him best I can but, well—here's a thought though—what say I give you the day off, Steven—"

"It is my day off," Steven says, collecting our plates as he gets up.

"Then where the bloody hell do you think you're going with that—Hilda's on breakfast—Hilda!—or do you want to put the poor girl out of a job?"

"I'll just take these through."

"Apologies, apologies, what else can I say?" Clive's voice drops a little, then bounces up, "Now here *is* a thought! What's say

145

I give Steven *and* your Uncle Clive both the day off—Hilda will hold the fort—and we treat our most distinguished guest to … what will we treat you to?"

"I was s'posed to be somewhere—" Steven says, coming back through.

"Somewhere! Somewhere! Anywhere in particular or just somewhere? I'd like to know more about these somewheres you get to and I don't doubt our guest would—"

"Walk with me to the stop, Sal?"

"Charming!" Clive commends Steven. "Bloody charming— walk me to the stop? Look here, I did not give you the day off so you could leave your sister standing at a bloody bus stop."

Clive's way. Steven's way. Just their way, that was all. So then, I'd get my coat, walk him to the stop and remember not to say anything about last night, about seeing Lawrence, about the cards and my hand and the face not his face that I hadn't been quite able to see—no, wouldn't say—had said I wouldn't, promised I wouldn't—but then I hadn't seen him—least not the Lawrence from that first year—Lawrence no more that Lawrence than Steven that Steven—no, so wouldn't say since hadn't seen—and remember not to ask Steven where he'd been or where he was going or who he was meeting or what he was doing and I'd be wondering if I could pass on that Hello from Dad and Steven would roll himself a cigarette so I'd hold on to that Hello and the bus would come too soon so I'd finish the cigarette, Dad's Hello left unsaid and, only once he'd gone, wonder why he didn't have his bike—why didn't he have his bike?—but at least he'd have gone before I forgot about remembering what not to ask, what not to say—just that it had brightened up, but then they had said it would—

"Cold though," Steven says, "aren't you cold?"

146

"No, maybe a bit—not really, no." I pull the gloves out of my pockets, "Want these?"

Steven smiles his half smile, laughs his half laugh. "So that's where they got to—"

"Clive's—"

"Technically—no, no, you keep them."

"Fine," I say, putting them on. I smile a half smile for myself, half for Lawrence—so they were Steven's—Lawrence wouldn't be going halves on smiles—I could keep it—he'd been quite serious about the gloves—they were Stevie's and that was that. I stretch my hands out to tempt Steven's reconsideration. "Freeze, if you like—"

"Thanks."

I take them off, holding the pair towards him. That half smile again. And me. Something.

"Oh, Clive's alright," he says, taking the gloves off me.

"I know."

"He's just a bit—hey, cross here, Sal, stop's just up there, we can walk along the front—not that it matters, doubt I'll be there all that much longer anyway—"

"But he's so—he's really very fond of you—"

"I'd better be careful not to tell him you said that." Corner of his mouth reaching up? Just—enough to let me give up a half laugh. Corner of his mouth turning back—holding on to his half. "Maybe—I suppose—it was only ever meant to be for a bit."

"But you'll be staying in Brighton?" Came out alright but still, that mess I'd gone and made of things last year makes a little nip—just to remind me—telling me I'd best keep a watch over what might slip out next—*stuck*, I'd said last year—hadn't meant it like that—Steven saying I was one to talk—couldn't help but think he did mean it like that—*stuck*—a whole year ago and still the word nipped—

"Oh, I don't know, Sal—"

"Do you think you might come back—" I try to pull the question back up by the scruff of its neck before it pounces but Steven's face tells me that it already had, its unspoken remainder scratching me as I see it scratch him—

Tap—

There it is, gone so faint but here again now, the beat winding its way up again right where it should have been so still—the sea's breath over us and—was meant to be still, meant to be soothed so close to the sea—

Steven's eyes are pressing on up the road, trying to make out what bus it is, his feet, eager to catch up with his eyes, quickening before they halt. "Wrong one," he says, pocketing his gloved hands as he turns to me.

"I don't know, OK Sal. I don't know." He might not be moving now but his eyes are pressing on again, reaching the stop, boarding the bus that would take him to wherever that somewhere was but no, he didn't know—about Clive, about Brighton, about coming back—coming back, coming home—at least I'd stopped before I'd gone and said that—might as well have—he'd heard it anyway when it's not like I'd really even consider it—at least not now—no, by now he was settled in my mind in Brighton—knew those boxes he'd left were probably all there'd ever be of Steven in that house, at least until—until what? There was no until—the boxes and the Hellos Dad would or wouldn't give me to pass on—those Hellos the only mention of him, just never came up—or never let ourselves bring it up—and my mother, swaddled by now in her infancy,

148

wouldn't say—try to remember the last time my mother said his name—had she said it since he'd left? Craved him when he was little, couldn't bear it when he started school, would always be taking his temperature, saying he couldn't go, or if he wanted to stay with a friend, but now? Filter his name in her voice from the last four years … yes—when was it now?, saying how nice it was that he was doing so well for himself, and a few times insisting we kept the line free since Steven must be trying to call—no, no she hadn't said that, she'd said "My son is trying to call," and then her calling the operator telling them they had to check the line, "My son is trying to call but there's been no call—there must be something wrong with the line, yes I'll wait—I'll"—then mixing her son up with her father—"My father is trying to call," she'd be telling the operator, "from Vienna," calling to tell her he'd found his way home, calling to tell her everything was going to be OK, her son was—but other than that, no—sure Dad must have wondered to himself—perhaps—best not of course, best not to wonder—and I hadn't—I don't—not anymore—just if he wanted, if he needed—his room was still there—his room and those boxes and—

"Still there," I say, straining a laugh after the words skip out, Steven's eyes snapping back from their point on the bus stop. "What?"

"Your room—it's still—"

"Well, I didn't imagine it had gone anywhere." The soured edges of his voice skin the soles of those skipping words, trip them into a stutter, and that laugh—that hideous forced laugh stripped, trying to hide now as it hears itself again.

"Look," he says—

"I'm sorry, I—"

"No look—"

"What?" The demand strikes out and swerves back at me.

"It's not like I live there anymore."

No. What he'd left. What I'd brought. Beating through him as it beat through me. Always thinking he'd never felt a—that raw throb, that pulse from infant to mother and back, the beat of waiting and not waiting, in that house, out here, in me. Of course he'd felt it—and of course he couldn't go back to it, he'd had to try, at least, to leave it—and maybe he had. Saying that about his room—why?—I hadn't meant anything by it— just—not that there was any question he would—not after four years—even I'm not that—I hadn't meant that at all. I'd meant London. Yes, that was what I'd meant. London.

The twitch, the quiver, the tick, the—

Tap—

There. Again there. The beat winding itself up right where and right when it should have been still, there again now when it had been so faint, hadn't seemed to follow me down once I'd closed the door to room five, seemed to have gone the way of those toys and their world and the dreams in rings around it: dissolved into silence, they melted by morning— and this morning the beat too—the beat of the infant-mother that throbbed the rhythm of nights and days and beat time for all the time between, time beaten timeless by the beat of the infant-mother tap tapping the toy drum hung round her baby neck, baby fists gripped round toy drumsticks—seemed it and she—but there it was again—

Tap—

There, again there—the infant-mother still clutching tight, still tapping, her beat still keeping time when morning came to melt those worlds away with the same cold red sun telling the same lie—

See over towards the shore now, those little floating isles already forging, gulls swooping to finish the breakfasts they'd left, little laughing, little floating—and there, the morning counterpart to last night's puppet, a man hunched over his metal detector, plodding and stalling, bending and checking.

"Find a penny pick it up ..." Steven's saying the words alone but I can hear our grandfather's voice behind it, following Steven's when it used to be Steven's voice catching up with our grandfather's—Steven sees the man with the metal detector, hunched, seeing what I see, seeing our grandfather bend and check—

"And all the day ..." It's my turn.

"Always stacked his coppers into those towers, remember?"

"Always took the top one off for you."

"Bernie's a millionaire!"

"A billionaire!"

"A trillionaire!" We say the last together, share out a laugh.

The bus stop is only a step or so away now and we're both leaning over the railings, both of us looking over the shore, just watching this man as he goes, plodding and stalling, bending and checking—

"I suppose you think—" Something else in Steven's voice now, stamping out a hollow where our grandfather's echo might have been—

"No I don't—"

"You do—"

"What—?" What? What did I think?

"Oh, just—never mind," stamping me out, stamping himself out too.

The man with metal detector is crouching right down, digging his hands under the pebbles, he pauses, straightens himself—seems to be holding something towards the sun.

"I wonder if they ever really find anything," Steven says, bringing himself back, bringing us all back. He leans a little further over the railings. "Listen," he says, turning towards me, "I've got to go and pick up my bike—won't be all that long I don't think, an hour maybe—"

"It's fine Steven—"

"Yeah, so I've got to—bit out of the way—" His eyes are going between his watch and the bus stop.

"Sure, of course—"

"Newhaven—it's—and then—well, then I've," his eyes just past me now. What was that stutter—that stutter wasn't his, didn't sound like his, makes me stiffen hearing him stutter—he was a mumbler yes, a mumbler and a mutterer but he didn't stutter, not like me—

"And then I've—" No, he didn't stutter, I want him to stop, I hadn't asked, he didn't have to say—no, not about where and what and who and now here he is, with a stutter that said I had made him—

"It's—well it's this—this chap—"

Chap. Chap? A laugh slips out of me—didn't mean to, couldn't be helped—where had that come from—a laugh that wasn't strained or forced or found—just fluttered up and slipped out. Steven's eyes had steadied on me. I hold them for a moment before I can answer them.

"Chap?" It's very nearly a genuine question.

"Alright, alright—anyway, I don't see what's wrong with chap," he says, my laugh, cheeky enough to flutter up again, nudges his defence, turning up a corner of his mouth, springing that half smile into a grin.

"Chap? No, nothing wrong with chap," I say—and I know that, for a moment at least, Steven's here, I'm here. "You can have chap if you like—"

"I do, particularly when it concerns this particular chap—"

"Particular to Newhaven—"

"What? Oh no, that's just Martin—"

"The bowler hat!" Giddy jump; cold plunge. Steven's eyes check me. I'm going to have to pull myself out. "Just a guess?" I try—but he knows my face better than that—five and eight again? Might have been Sal but he still knows that face.

Tell tell tell or I'll tell tell tell—

No. But still couldn't say, had the blink and the blur of Lawrence saying not to say, promising not to—only knew the bowler hat was Martin because of—

"Lawrence I ..." Too late to look down but I look down anyway—*promise is a promise is a*—can't unbreak a broken promise with looking down but I—

"Lawrence?" Yes, Steven still knows that face—my face—Sally's face—

"I wouldn't have known it was him, well maybe I would— but you mustn't say—I said wouldn't—just down there wasn't it?"

"What?"

"The shop—the chippie—I'm sure that's where it was."

"Was, yes—ages since—did I take you?—funny, I don't remember—bead shop now or something—Lawrence practically gave the place away—"

"But it was all boarded up."

"No that's further along—I'm trying to think—you sure you met Lawrence?—that must have been—"

"It was a while ago—"

"He was still ..." he was going to say something else—he was still Lawrence, I want him to say. He takes out his tobacco and rolls a cigarette.

"Is he alright?" Stutter-stop—wanting and not wanting to ask—wanting and not wanting to know—because somehow if Lawrence was alright then maybe Steven was alright and if Steven's alright then maybe—

"Sounds as thought you'd know better than me."

"I only saw him for a minute," I say, but I know it doesn't make any difference, I feel transparent, the ghosts inside me wishing themselves now inside safer skin—can't bear the home they never chose but cannot leave. Can't tell now what Steven can see, he's not looking at me but around him, at his watch, counting out something half aloud—"Steven are you—"

"What?"

"I mean Lawrence—" The sigh says he doesn't believe me-but it's easier to pretend that he does.

"Lawrence—yeah, he's—no—no. Twat. What time did you see him anyway?"

"I don't know. Ten maybe."

"Ten! Christ, maybe I should go straight to Lawrence's—if he's even there—what's left of him—bugger Martin—I should have known he'd screw up—"

"I don't understand," my words but it's Steven's eyes that blink, narrow—no, I do understand: this one isn't for understanding.

Steven shakes his head, looks away, "He's just not all that well, alright? But look, if you want to come—"

"To Newhaven?" Steven's face had caught the way it had that time I saw the beat catch hold in him—the dart, the grasp—not quite, not matched, it didn't lock—but enough to make me want to say—to reach a hand or an arm or just—without stuttering or stepping round—just ask: "Steven are you—"

"Fine! Christ, Sal!"

"Sorry, I'm—" Me looking down again and Steven's face god knows where and wondering how we got to this where it's all prickles and stutters and sorrys. Steven's face is squeezed out of sense and he doesn't look up as his hand reaches towards me, this jerky little nod drawing me into a stiff hug. "Sorry, Sal," he says. I find a half laugh to tell him to stop with the sorrys, that he's worse than me—

"Oh no," he says, "no one's worse than you." Half laughs each. Steven's face still pinched though. He gives my back a quick pat that tells me half laughs and hugs are over—alright, I want to say, it's alright, but I've said enough, almost too much before I'm too close.

"Come with me to Lawrence then, Sal—said I'd go, have to now I've said—you'll come though—he'd like that I think—"

"Stevie's sister?" I say, smiling, but a twitch in the brow tells me Steven doesn't remember—

"I'll have to go to Martin—check he gave Lawrence his meds and that—yes, and get my bike—got to get my bike and every-thing … You don't have to, only if you want—when I said he's not well, it's not like he's—I mean he's a really good—" Long breath and the closing eyes—

"Chap?" A smile for that. "No, I'd like to."

155

"Well, alright—but just don't say anything about it."

"What do you mean?" My question closes Steven's eyes again, as though he thinks I know when all I have is a couple of fragments from last night—Lawrence catching and dropping my hand, giving his own hands little slaps, saying whoever they were "made it all up". But I had more than that—not much, but a bit, enough—seen that somewhere between the Lawrence in the fish shop that first year and the fractured child-clown on the bench last night: humpty-dumpty had had his great fall and Steven hadn't been able to put him back together again. But I suppose Steven and I knew something about broken things—that sometimes you just couldn't mend them. Never stopped trying though. Because you can't—until you do: stop and leave the broken thing behind.

"Just don't—" Steven says. "I know you wouldn't but—it's just he's still a bit funny about it all, so just better not to say anything—second thought maybe I'd better just go round on my own, you wouldn't really want—"

"How do you know what—" I stop before skipping words ask to have their soles skinned again. They trip but I pick them up, holding them firmly until I hear fragments recorded in Lawrence's voice play, pause, replay—

Don't say—didn't see—made it all up—ask Stevie—never meant—

My skipping words tumble, breaking on the pavement—

Badbadnaughtynaughty—only wanted to hold—just for a moment—

The blink and blur of Lawrence's face again, his hand catching and dropping mine—ask Stevie, he'd said—ask what?—didn't want to—couldn't hear what might—not lose the Lawrence I'd remembered—couldn't lose him yet—lose that Lawrence, lose that Steven—

"What did he say, Sal?"

"Nothing."

Knew that face.

"That they made it all up."

"Made what all up?"

This was horrible—shouldn't have started, should never have said—hadn't seen—

Promise is a—

"He said to ask you." My eyes that are just past his now—his that see without seeing my face giving me away with no blink or blur or mix of lights to muddle it—I'd never seen that face, only the face it made Steven wear—setting his mouth, his eyes, closing him up, closing me off—

"Oh I don't know," he says, "all a bloody mess, my fault really—"

"No, it wasn't!"

"And you'd know, would you?"

It's not a question—I know it's not a question, because, of course, there is no answer—at least not one I can give—thumbnail, skirt pleat, shoelace—

"Sorry, Sal—just all such a bloody mess and wouldn't be if I'd stayed with Lawrence like I said I would—not like it would have been any skin off my nose—game of chess—not much to ask—and I could see Lawrence was having one of his—his days—blank days—days where he said it all just went ..."

"Went what?"

"That was—or is I suppose—it: blank—the days he just gets, I don't know, emptied out—says he gets emptied out—sorry, this must sound completely—"

"No, it doesn't—"

"Oh, Sal," he's looking down, I'm looking down—we're at the bus stop but we're also sitting at the end of our mother's bed, hearing her own sleep waking her, *Daddy*—

"It's OK, Mamma."

"Steven? Sally?"

"Point is," Steven says, looking up, "on blank days he has to close up early, that's the deal—well really it's me or Martin that's supposed to and take him home and that—and it was my day and it just would have to be the day that some bloke turns up, threatening, saying Lawrence better not go anywhere near his missus again or—would've been funny if it wasn't so—has all these questions for Lawrence—and I'm telling you, Sal, well, Lawrence is in that kind of state he couldn't recite a bloody nursery rhyme let alone improvise an alibi about some girl he'd never seen so next thing any of us know half of Brighton is after the rapist from the chip shop—"

"But that's ridiculous."

"Maybe, but it's the way it was, Sal."

They couldn't—he couldn't—not that Lawrence—not any Lawrence—saw those hands asking to be absolved—*OK, it's OK*—of course they'd made it all—

"And Lawrence has a night in a cell—doesn't sound much, but it was the way they went after him, and banging on the door of the chippie, the windows, tipped him—"

Humpty Dumpty had a great fall—

"Sort of over the—"

All the kings horses and all …

"He never laid a finger—honestly, Sal, he never—"

Runaway words, couldn't catch them, try to net them, stutter as bad as—

"Lawrence never—oh look, that's me—gotta—" Steven nodding to the bus coming towards the stop. "Bloody typical," he says, handing his cigarette to me.

"I would," I say, net falling over a catch I hadn't expected, "I'll come."

"What? With Lawrence in his filthy boxers in that filthy flat?"

Steven's getting out his pass, a caught sigh in his voice. "OK then," he takes the cigarette back off me for a last drag, "say an hour, an hour and a half to be safe. Burlington Street, it's the third on your left up there, Burlington Street, OK? Number eight—and don't—" But he's got to get on the bus, see you later, he's saying, corner of his mouth twitching—

Sure, number eight, see him later.

* * *

Burlington Street. Number eight. Hour and a half. Just hope Lawrence wouldn't be able to see that I'd said—Steven might know my face—that face—still the same face and still tied double bows—but Lawrence didn't know it—the one he'd pieced up that first year in the chippie—the one he'd tested last night with *a promise is a*—wish I hadn't—five and eight or twenty-eight it didn't matter—trail of broken promises and broken things from London to Brighton—Lawrence not that Lawrence, Steven not that Steven—but better not that than none at all—still the same Sally though under that Sal, still that face and double bows, still empty enough for—

No, not just now—the beating of the infant-mother still and the ghosts quiet—

Not too cold to sit on the beach for a bit is it? Start wandering about and only get myself lost. Know it's third on the left from here. Can't see the man with his metal detector now—or is that him there, made his way right up near the carousel, scavenging along with the gulls—was that him? Steven saw it in him too—that bending and checking—the way our grandfather had—wanted the infant-mother to see it too, see it was alright—just what they did, had to be done, practical, preparing for the journey, home safe, home sound—well of course they must find something. Wouldn't keep at it like that if they didn't—

Doesn't look like the Golden Gallopers have had any takers yet, too early maybe, but there they are, still gliding up and down, the carousel going round and round with or without riders to squeal, leaning high up as they dared before rushing over the pebbles and down to the water, plunging before the cold had time to scare you out, giggling and shivering and the sea, with or without them, now as then, still drawing its expectant breath in back towards the horizon.

* * *

"Sorry, Sal," Steven says, going up the front step to press the bell, "didn't think it would take that long."

"It's nice here," I say, glancing up towards where I'd strayed, "there's a butcher's, a baker's—"

"Candlestick maker's—you've seen the sights then—oh come on, Lawrence—"

"You only just rang it," I say as Steven reaches for the bell again. He steps back, straining his neck up. "So it's like that, is it?" Steven's asking the second storey window.

"What?"

"He's got the bloody curtains closed again," he says, familiarising me with Lawrence's reluctance to let the day inside.

"We could come back later, get a cup of tea or something—" but Steven is already back up the step, his finger holding down the bell until a shrill blurt jumps out of the speaker, beating the impatient finger away—

"Whad'y'want?" The squawk throws a cold flannel across our faces. Steven mouths that it's Lawrence's mother before he manages to pull out his name. There's a pause of crackles and then, barging past it, a blaring "Lawrence!"

"It's her place," Steven says as a merciful buzz releases the door.

"His mother's?"

"Mrs Sergeant, yeah."

"Not Corporal Major?" I ask, picturing the dramatisation Clive had offered us the evening before.

"What? Oh ignore all that—that's just—"

"Clive?"

"Yeah," a half smile makes its concession. "She's really not that bad—did one of those buy to let things and I managed to talk her into the idea of Lawrence having it for a bit, just till he'd pulled himself together—he was meant to be out months ago—"

"I'll bleedin' say he was," the squawk comes from the next flight up where Mrs Sergeant, rubber-gloved, has interrupted her scrubbing to welcome Steven and "What's this you've brought with you?"

"Mrs Sergeant," Steven hastily polishes his voice, "meet my sister."

"Sally," I offer my name and hand together, trying to pair up the immaculate bun and lipless mouth with Clive's account. Mrs Sergeant's hand, still rubber gloved, snatches mine.

"Pauline," Mrs Sergeant matches a mock curtsey with a sweetened tone. She holds the maid's pose for a moment then snaps upright, sending a fierce blast over her shoulder, "Lawrence! Visitors!" She's pulling her rubber gloves a little tighter up her arms as she turns back to glance us over. "Well," she says, her voice sticking where the dose of syrup had been drained, "you couldn't have chosen a better time. Mind you shut the door behind you."

Granted entry, we trail after Mrs Sergeant's giddy stomp inside where washing is piled on the sofa, chairs, and table beneath a confusion of wooden dogs, newspapers, picture frames dropped face down and two lamps whose shades are held like top hats by each bared plump arm of the sofa. Mrs Sergeant pours the contents of various amber potions into a bucket and her arm disappears. "You won't mind standing," she says, her arm reappearing with a sponge before picking up the bucket and slapping her feet to the wall hung with damp-mottled ovals and oblongs which the pictures had dressed. "Walls want a good scrubbing—whole sty wants a good scrubbing for that matter." She pounces on Steven's glance at the chairs, "there'll be nowhere to sit till I've got these walls scrubbed—if you don't like it, well—" My incautious eye had just landed on Mrs Sergeant's sponge, making its proprietor seize—"A good scrub is what these walls want, and this floor—if he", she said, snout directed towards the closed door across the hall, "wants to go rolling about in his own muck—well, I won't have it—he," she says, stabbing a rubber gloved finger snoutwards, "he could do with a good scrub himself—little piglet—no, I won't have it." Mrs Sergeant drops the sponge back into the bucket. "I won't have it, I won't," and, eyes on the closed door now, she stomps the three or four steps to it to inflict a single bang with her rubber gloved fist. "That should do it," she says with a wink, performing a delicate half step back and cupping a rubber-gloved hand round an ear, "Helloo there! Is anybody hoo-oom?" The door returns her serenade with a silence that confiscates her wink, forcing the rubber-gloved fist to repeat itself. "You unlock that door this minute or I'll bash it in I will!"

I hear Steven take a sharp breath but, seeing his eyes half closed, drop mine to the ground and there, mimicking Steven's, find refuge in the lashed half dark. We shouldn't be here. We'd mixed up the tickets. This isn't what we're supposed to be seeing. No good trying that one—I'd had my warning—skimmed it off though, skimmed last night off too—peeled away whatever wouldn't tally, whatever admitted that Lawrence wasn't that Lawrence, that Steven wasn't that Steven—still telling myself that *not that* was better than none at all—as though I might believe a word of my own lies, feel the sting of them now though as Mrs Sergeant's rubber-gloved hands smack together—Mrs Sergeant who had, as though quite unexpectedly, launched herself centre stage. She seemed to be considering her position. She surveyed her audience and allowed a smile: yes, she would be heard, she would be seen—and it was Steven and this Sally girl who would see.

No, we wouldn't—or at least I wouldn't—I shouldn't be here—not to see, to watch—not this.

The opening door denies Mrs Sergeant's rubber-gloved fist its third bang.

Smudged and faded, the lines that had drawn the Lawrence in front of us all now seem to have been made some time ago, another rough draft the hand couldn't bring itself to finish. The image of the Lawrence I met last night is no longer there to skim away but the Lawrence I want to remember is almost here, just discernible where he'd been rubbed out—could just

163

trace the sketches between that Lawrence and the Lawrence now lifting his head for a moment as he comes in, his towelling robe coming undone, eyes flicking past his mother to Steven, to me and back to Steven again.

"Well, good bleedin' mornin'," Mrs Sergeant says, arms folded, voice well settled back into its squawk. "Aren't you going to say hello?"

Lawrence nods at Steven, eyes on then off me, and goes over to one of the chairs, bundling its contents on top of the pile already on the table before pulling out the chair, one hand securing it, the other opening towards me.

"Please," he says—could he see? He won't look at me, only at the chair—*don't say*—*didn't see*—*promise is a*—seems for a moment he might be keeping the promise for me but this acknowledgement of my presence, this invitation, recalls nothing, bypassing last night, letting me off—if no one had seen then no promise could have been made and if no promise had been made then no promise could be broken—

"Please," the repetition is immaculate and he's looking up at me now, face as clear and present as his single word that holds nothing but a sliver of this moment: me and his hand that needs no absolving on the back of the chair; everything else recedes.

"Oh, so he can speak," Mrs Sergeant says. "Listen to it! Thought the cat had y' tongue. Come and give your mother a kiss." Lawrence doesn't move though, he just goes on standing behind the chair, eyes hovering on Steven now.

"Go on, Sal," Steven says from behind ventriloquist lips. I look from Steven to Lawrence whose eyes are trying to fix themselves to the seat of the chair. Mrs Sergeant stomps to it, sits: "Now give your mother a kiss, I'm not a leper. Scared the life out your mother you did, in there, not a sound—I thought you were dead, thought I'd be bashing the door in to find

164

you rotting—lord almighty, what would I 'ave said? They'd all think I'd done it! Killed my own in cold blood! Well, you almost did me in with the fright—kiss y'ma now, come on." The imperatives land weightless on Lawrence as he drifts over to the window and takes up the pack of cards on the sill.

"I said give your mother a kiss." Mrs Sergeant does not want to change strategy but, sitting with her rubber-gloved hands folded on her lap, she experiments with clicking a tongue and waits. She stretches her neck a little to one side and waits. She turns an expectant cheek up and waits. "Excuse him," she says after a snort, spooning the syrup over her voice for the benefit of those two words alone and then, with a flamboyant toss of her head, levers herself up to jab her finger into Lawrence's back. "You're rude!" she blasts. "Rude, rude, rude! Do you know what you are? Hmm? Do you? I'll tell you: rude, rude, rude!" And with each chant comes another jab. I judder at each but Lawrence hardly seems to move.

"Maybe we should go," I whisper to Steven.

"What was that?" Mrs Sergeant lurches round, locking my eyes with a glare. The key is dangling—say something, I will have to say—

"Sally was just saying," Steven snatches the dangling key for me. "Sally was just saying how nice you're ... things are," he's trying to turn the key, unlock my eyes from Mrs Sergeant's glare, only to get himself convicted.

"Things?"

Running with their unanticipated chance of escape, my eyes, while seeming to be held by a spot on the floor just beyond my feet, race back the way they had come: down the stairs, down the street, along the front—

"My things?"

165

The glare takes us both into custody now. My eyes dash back: along the front, up the street, up the stairs, noting once again all the washing had made a bed for—the frames, the lamps, the dogs. Now that my eyes have returned with the goods they at once assume the position of their blind representatives that had been left fixed on the floor—up they come and with them a splutter of—

"Dogs!"

"I beg your pardon!" Mrs Sergeant splutters back.

"Your dogs, they're lovely!" An exchange of grace for haste waves my hand at the wooden dogs on the washing. Only two. I thought there'd been more. Steven's cheek is unusually animated—surely a chuckle waiting inside it. "Lovely!" I can't believe I've said it again—can't look up at Steven— can't look anywhere—eyes end up just where they shouldn't: Mrs Sergeant—though, for a moment, the glare seems to dim a little, yes, lets me blur—only a moment though—Mrs Sergeant's working up a squeeze and scrunch of her face, her glare blazing to be appreciated it in all its glory.

"I", Mrs Sergeant slaps a splayed fingered hand over her chest, "think dogs smell." With that she switches the glare off and I'm sure any moment Steven's chuckle will have its way but instead a silence casts its skin down, waking the infant-mother as it falls over the four of us—four made five, the infant-mother crawling between us, crawling beneath the fallen skin, stretching it taut to make herself a new drum. With its flayed skin tight, the silence hands the infant-mother her sticks to drum its beat and repeat the beat of silence itself: beating, repeating, each beat repeats the last, beating back to beat on and on to beat back, time bound by silence, silence bound by time, time tied to silence, kept still, made timeless, held fast over the drum—

Unless—

Or until—

Something—

Or someone—

Yes, if someone—

Or something—

Only there's no one—

There's nothing—

Only sticks beating—

Repeating—

Unless—

Or until—

Hear that?

Nothing—

Thought it might—

No—

Be someone, be something, heard it—

Almost—

Remote but definite—not yet someone—or a voice even—not quite, no—no, it was still just a sound, a sound starting, trying, to sound itself into a voice, a voice starting, trying, to sound itself into being, sounding itself against the silence, no word though, not yet—didn't mean it wasn't saying something though—and less remote now too—yes, but less distinct some- how, losing its definition as it found a shape and the shape a speaker: "I", it's saying, "I"—it's Lawrence, his unpractised tongue rehearsing with a quiet diligence, shaping sound into an "I" that seemed apart from him—an "I" whose speaker did not own it, unconscious of its effect, its offering, unaware that sounding itself should gently loose time from silence and lift the skin from the drum, wrapping it round the infant, the mother, the good infant-mother—she curls up foetal now, curled up, wrapped up, baby fists open and toy drumsticks drop: sound shaped against silence loosing time to beat on.

I looked at Lawrence, his gently dishevelled earnestness and the sight of him, the completeness of his sincerity, shamed me—who had I been to say what was and wasn't broken?

"I—" Lawrence starts again

"What? You bleedin' what?" The apparently senseless lull has given new potency to Mrs Sergeant's blast. "What's all this I-I-I?—aye-aye! What? Are you a bloody pirate or something?"

Lawrence turned to face us, blinking eyes coming up only to scramble away out of the glare whose assistance Mrs Sergeant once again requires. Lawrence's eyes come back and steady themselves just above Steven. He takes a moment, raising his caved chest and says with an assurance that flickers of the Lawrence I had met that first year, the Lawrence behind that counter, a Lawrence who seemed twice the size of the Lawrence standing here now in his tea-stained robe, eyes just over Steven's head, saying—

"I like dogs."

"You what?" Mrs Sergeant is yapping at me as though I hold the explanation for her son's incomprehensible announcement. Dogs. If only I had come up with something else.

"I like dogs. I think", and here he blinks at me, "that dogs smell … OK." His conclusion snaps the yapping mouth shut—but also leaves Steven unable to keep hold of his chuckle, a chuckle that tickles playmates for itself out of me and then, worse, Lawrence—Lawrence whose laughing mouth has caught the rest of his face off guard. Catching up, Lawrence's face begins laughing along, his whole body following—except the one hand clutching his belly. It seems he's having to endure these convulsions, as inexplicable to him as they are to his mother. Mrs Sergeant, immune to this contagion, tightens her decidedly unamused mouth before it dares gape at this horrifying reconfiguration of her son; her cheeks, radiant with puce fury, immediately drink themselves white. The back of a rubber-gloved hand is brought to her forehead, held there as she waits for her posture to take the desired effect. Nothing. She sneaks a peek and reassumes her downward gaze, her mouth softening just a touch as she hears my chastened laugh scurry away, softening a touch more as Steven's chuckle sidles off. But Lawrence, her boy, utterly riddled by it! She can hardly bear to look at him—riddled! Possessed! A rubber-gloved palm pressed over a galloping heart. Mrs Sergeant drops into the chair, sighs, sighs again, and, overcome with sighing, begins consulting both sides of her rubber-gloved hands. "All for what?" She's hissing through her teeth, looking up at us all, then, exclusively, irreparably, on Lawrence.

"All for what? Hmm?" And with each tug at the tips of her rubber-gloved fingers Lawrence's uproarious spasms subside. His brows furrow as he wipes his nose with the back of his hand.

"Hmm?"

Lawrence sniffs, his eyes and head down, dislocating himself from the eyes drawn towards him: mine, Steven's, Mrs Sergeant's—but he is looking at the no-man's-land just in front of his feet. My eyes drift towards it, Steven's too, but it's not ours—the eyes catch and recede, as though they might be able to find and settle on a no-man's-land of their own.

"Having a laugh at your mother's expense now are we?" she asks with a clenched smile, tongue forked to splice geniality with ferocity. "Taking the P out of your ma?" The rubber gloves are ripped off and slapped down on the table which, under the heaped washing, buffers her aim, ensuring the gloves a well cushioned landing. The glare must be enlisted once again, this time to reprimand the washing that had mocked her efforts; the gloves, inside out, flop bloated, white, fingerless.

No—no, I shouldn't be here—I should have gone—before, I should—

Mrs Sergeant turns her head away to address an absent but thoroughly sympathetic listener, "He takes the P he does. Me, his Ma, I'm ashamed, ashamed of my own," then, lurching back round to tell Lawrence: "You should be ashamed of y'self. Anyone else would have had them put you away—but not your Ma. No, your honour, his Ma will look after him." A pause is admitted, the emptiness of which throws Mrs Sergeant's face into her hands, "Oh my boy, my boy," wailing with a dry sob as she gets up and lunges towards him, crushing herself against his inertia, his arms and head dangling unresponsive to all the maternal force Mrs Sergeant can exert. The seconds protract before she unpeels herself, her finger compelled to have a poke at Lawrence's immobility. "Gone all quiet again, have we? So you should. Don't know why I didn't just have 'em put you away. Should've just let them keep you banged up a bit longer, shouldn't I? Let them stick you in the loony bin. How would you like that? Eh? Wouldn't let you get way with taking the P, they wouldn't, wouldn't let you sit around all grubby either, make you clean yourself up, they would, they would you know and if you didn't … they'd scrub you themselves, scrub you raw, they would, scrub you so hard you'd wish you'd never been born—you'll be crying for y'ma then, I can tell you." Mrs Sergeant's snort has lost its relish: "No child of mine, he's not," she tells her absent listener, and then, turning her head aside, she says confidentially, "Should've had them put him away." The absent ear, with reliable pity, had to agree. Mrs Sergeant is now at liberty to prolong a satisfying sigh before she begins her laboured course towards the hall. "I suppose I'll just go then, shall I?" her squawk pivots round to us.

All of us.

"Just go. Just leave. Not even a goodbye," she says, pulling on her coat, "see, I'm going now, I'm—don't you even want to know where y'ma's going? Hmm? No? Well, fine. I am being taken out for luncheon. Sir Martin is taking your Lady Ma out for lunch-ee-owne—I'll see what he's got to say about all this—all his hard work—if it weren't for Martin I'd be bringing you ciggies on a Sunday just like I had to do for your Pa—" As her mouth snaps shut her eyes needle Steven and me, then, bristling, her squawk gulped down, she hisses at me: "You never been told it's rude to stare?"

Well, Little Miss?

Yes—yes of course—but I hadn't been staring—hadn't so much as looked up, didn't dare—my eyes make a futile clutch for any spot of no-man's-land on the floor—shouldn't have come—shouldn't have seen—but I had and Mrs Sergeant had made an audience out of me like it or not. She's got her coat and hat on now, leaving her hiss in our ears behind her as she closes the door—gone but not gone and yet still here I am, my eyes skittering for a spot on the floor as though there was some way out of the fact that I'd come and I'd seen and Lawrence had seen himself seen. I want Steven to say something, for Lawrence to look up, break the cell walls dividing us.

But Steven doesn't say anything and Lawrence doesn't look up, just says, with his head still down, quite mechanically, as though he's proposing an answer to a hypothesis:

"No, you shouldn't laugh at people." Quite flat, he says it and gives a small but deliberate nod.

"No one's laughing at anyone," Steven says, echoing Lawrence's hollow tone.

"It's not nice to laugh at people."

"No."

"It's not nice to take the P."

"No one's taking the P—"

"Yes you were!" Lawrence fires, his head spurting up, milky eyes beginning to well. "Yes you were! And it's not nice. It's not nice to go taking the P out of Ma." Steven tries moving towards Lawrence, putting his hand on his shoulder.

"I didn't mean to be laughing," Lawrence says, lowering his head again. "I didn't mean anything—I don't—and they can't bang me up—not like Martin keeps saying, like Ma—don't let them bang me up, Stevie—"

"Don't talk like that—no one's going to—"

"Or put me away—I didn't do anything—never—only wanted—just for a moment—all I—" Lawrence shakes Steven off, wiping his hands on his towelling robe. "Didn't—never—all I—"

"I know that—we know that," Steven says, looking at me. "We know that, don't we, Sal?" I'm nodding, nodding too hard, too much, but it raises Lawrence's head, or, it seems to be what raises it—he's squinting his eyes between Steven and me.

"I don't know why I was laughing," he says, letting his head hinge limply from his neck, turning it a little to each side as though he might find an explanation on one. "I don't know," he tells the ground between him and Steven. With his head up

172

a little, Lawrence's eyes seem to be trying to rest on Steven, they hover, still squinting, flickering again before they resign themselves back to the floor.

"Why don't you put your glasses on, Lawrence?" Steven tries. "Always better with your specs on." Looks as though they've been through this one before.

Lawrence shakes his head, "Can't find 'em," he says.

"Is that right?"

"No idea where they are."

Steven's giving himself up to his half smile.

"Gone walkabout," Lawrence says. "Gone missing."

"Is that right?"

"No, this time they really are, promise Stevie, I had 'em— them—on, I had them on, I was doing the cards and that last night when you'd gone, left 'em on the table and when I come back today they've gone." Soldier straight, Lawrence folds his arms, and with his eyes straight at Steven, blinks. Steven takes what must be the prescribed slow motion steps to the table, lifts the bundle of washing—"These what you're after?"

"Magic!" Lawrence says, beaming as he puts them on.

"Oh, I think your ma gets the credit for this one—" Steven stops, his half smile disowned, slithering off to take cover as Lawrence's beam fades, a glare not his own hardening behind bespectacled eyes, locking Steven's without a blink or a flicker, defending the name of the law.

"I'm sorry, Lawrence." Steven's attempting to do what he can to neaten the bundles on the table but the glare in Lawrence's eyes disappears as fast as the beam had faded and now he's letting his head drop again, tightening his robe, turning away.

He sits down at the table, pushes the bundles aside with his forearm, letting Steven's efforts tumble to the floor as he picks up the cards to shuffle and cut with a sense of duty that seals him apart from the room. I try to gauge Lawrence by Steven, by his half smile slithering back and off again, seeing him leaning forward a little now, retracting his words before they're spoken.

"Tell you what, Lawrence," Steven risks at last, "you give us this week's lottery numbers and I'll make you a sandwich."

"Shut up, Stevie," Lawrence says without looking up. "You don't know anything about this stuff."

"There's nothing I don't know about making the world's best ham sandwich." Steven's cringing as he moulds a face that might partner this strain at the avuncular.

"I said shut up, Stevie."

"Sal, isn't it true I make the world's best—tell Lawrence how I—"

"Sure," I want to say, "the best," but it doesn't come out aloud. Steven mouths an irritable *thanks* and rolls his eyes.

"Shut up, shut up, shut up." Lawrence's voice flicks out as he smacks the heel of his hand against his forehead.

"OK, OK—just thought maybe—" Steven's looking at me, gives up, looks back to Lawrence. "I'll just make myself a bite then—and Sal?"

I nod—but I shouldn't be nodding—I should be going—should never have come—leave now, not make things any worse at least—

"OK," Steven says, letting his breath go, testing his half smile, offering it to me. "Lawrence, you sure I can't—"

"Not hungry, Stevie."

"Well, just give me a shout if you change your mind."

"Doesn't matter," Lawrence mutters through a huff and turns over the first card. "All bollocks anyway."

"No, it's not," Steven says.

"Shut up, Stevie. I know you think it's all a load of bollocks. You think it's bollocks. Ma thinks it's bollocks. S'pose you—" Lawrence is taking aim, eyes on me. I shake my head—of course I don't think—Lawrence lets himself consider this possibility before he returns his focus to the cards. "But it's not," he tells them, "it's not bollocks."

"Right then," Steven begins, the bland conviction dimly punctuating the last of this episode as he lays his feet down towards the next.

"Where are you going?" Lawrence's urgency springs his head up from his cards and round towards Steven.

"Just to make a bite," Steven says, each word checked on the scale, "make you something too if you like—"

"What you making?"

"Sandwiches."

"Oh."

"Do you want one?"

"No thanks, Stevie."

"Sure?"

"Yes, Stevie," Lawrence says and both resume their course, one taking his steps, the other turning, considering his cards. "What kind of sandwiches?" Lawrence was simply making enquiries, nothing more.

"Ham."

"Ham sandwiches?"

"Yes, Lawrence, ham, I'm making me and Sal ham sandwiches."

"I like ham sandwiches. Sometimes with tomato. Sometimes not."

"So I'll make you a ham sandwich."

"With tomato or not with tomato?"

It's as though Steven's being asked to guess which hand. "Not with?"

"Not with ... OK Stevie, make me a ham sandwich."

My eyes measure a spot on the floor. No-man's is the most they can conclude.

"You're Stevie's sister," Lawrence suggests.

"That's right," I say, meeting his bravery.

"Stevie's sister, Sally." He's piecing me together again, leaning back for that first year as I had and, reaching back to see himself as he was, lets me see Steven as he was, organising each of us in turn into familiarity.

I nod, smile, Lawrence nods, smiles, scratches the corner of his mouth. Don't look down again—holding the thought for Lawrence as much as for myself—I needn't have—no, Lawrence is rediscovering all the advantages of bespectacled eyes—determined, they hold themselves steady.

"You came to the shop," he says. "You came with Stevie. You came—I remember you—you came with Stevie for fish and chips. You came and ..." I might have skimmed last night off but Lawrence, with a simple absence of acknowledgement, had looked past it, blotted it out—hadn't seen—no. No promise made to be broken. His trailing voice might have confessed, admitted his words were a repetition. I watch his hands clench and release, unsure of the next turning as he sucks in and puffs out his cheeks. I should say something, bring us back on course—hardly doing my bit, can't be fair—not right my being there at all, but now that I am I might at least try and chip in with something—

"And now you've come here," Lawrence tells me, his smile broadening as the way presents itself—"Magic!"—no, he didn't need me to chip in—but still—feel I really should offer something—answer his smile—

"Yes—I hope you don't mind ..."—so that was chipping in, was it? Was that what I'd called doing my bit? Well, if doing my bit meant inverting the very smile I'd wanted to answer—just when I could see he didn't need me to go chipping in, I'd gone and chipped in all the same—

"About what?" Lawrence's eyes flickering behind his specs, two knuckles drawing themselves across his forehead—oh, why go chipping in when a smile back would do? Why, when a smile and a nod which, on every other occasion never failed to prove their inadequacy, would—for once—suffice?

"Mind about what? What would I mind about? I don't mind about ... anything."

The smile and the nod then. Lawrence returns the gesture, consults the map, retracing a step or two to go on—

"Yes, and now you've come here, come with Stevie, come to visit me—that's nice. I like visitors," he pauses to amend, "so long as they're Stevie—or—Stevie's sister."

"I'm Stevie's sister!" I grin what I know must be a ridiculous grin—Stevie? I never called—

"Stevie!" Lawrence beams as Steven comes back in, "this is your sister, Sally!"

177

Steven catches his laugh, puts the plate of sandwiches on the table and says yes, that's right, this is Sally, my sister Sally and that there's not any ham after all.

"Oh," Lawrence frowns, "no ham."

"'Fraid not. Not much of anything. Lucky dip it is—this one's some sort of spread, this one's ..."

"I don't want any—" Lawrence starts.

"Jam, this one's—", Steven brings it up to his nose and takes a cautious sniff. "No, I don't think I want any either," he admits, half smile pinching a cheek. "I'd better go and get you some supplies."

"No. No going out," Lawrence says.

"Lawrence, there's one manky-looking apple and a bit of bread—"

"It's OK, Stevie, I was never that hungry anyway—"

"Well I am! Don't be a prat—"

"I'm not a prat!"

"You'll have to eat at some point."

"Who says?"

Steven turns to me. "Perhaps you should—" With a slight raise of his eyes Steven glances towards the door. I mimic the same and it's only then that I notice I've had my coat on all this time—all this time when I should have been gone—should never have come—and Steven did say—bit late for all that—just make the best of the worst with the nod and the smile and be out the door and down the stairs, on my way back the way I'd come as though I'd never come at all—never come, never stayed, never seen—helped along by Steven's eyes advising my steps to the door, showing me out and my own eyes matching the fact of the matter, understanding that of course I had no business still being here, understanding that "perhaps" of his for the imperative it hardly pretended not to be and yet still—still!—still standing here in the coat I'd never taken off, making Steven's eyes repeat themselves with increasing emphasis, going from me to the door and back, Lawrence's eyes, bespectacled but squinting nonetheless, working hard to resolve this silent exchange, blinking from me to the door to Steven to me.

"Really nice to see you again," I say, finding myself a step towards Lawrence rather than the door.

"Yeah," Lawrence is working his nails round a relatively clean patch of his towelling robe—say something else should I?

"See you later then, Sal."

No. Nothing else. I follow Steven's prompt before my eyes or feet stall me, trying to make room for a goodbye.

"No," Lawrence says, turning me back round. "What did I say? I said no going out."

Steven's thumb and index finger rub his forehead. I wait for the rolling eyes, the sigh.

"I knew you thought it was all bollocks," Lawrence says with fierce satisfaction. "I knew it!"

"I do not think anything's bollocks. I think I need to get you and me something to eat."

"No you don't—"

"And I think Sal needs to get going—"

"Why?"

"Because she does—"

"Where? She can't. She's only just come, she's … my visitor. She came with you to visit me and—and I like visitors and—" The spread of cards make their claim, cutting him out, standing him up, ensuring his loyalty before they allow him to go on. He gives the cards their nod, gives Steven his: "If you go—if you make her go—then you do think it's all bollocks."

Steven's whole hand is clawing his head now. "Fine," he says, "fine. So we'll all just stay here, shall we?"

"Yes. We'll all stay here."

"Indefinitely."

"Yes."

"Wonderful."

"Unless," Lawrence says, his turn to set his words on the scales, "un-le-ess we all go to the beach together!" The exclamation makes the scales teeter and Lawrence tips them with another, speeding on, "No! Not the beach—the pier! You, me, Stevie's sister—all of us! And I'll do the cards," he says, grabbing my hand. "Just get my boots—"

I had thought Steven was about to speak but he just gives the sigh that seems to have become his.

"Get my boots, my scarf—get my scarf, Stevie—please?—Show Stevie's sister the talking telescope."

Half smiles each. "Oh, Sally knows all about the talking telescope."

"But this one's special, this one—"

"Talks?"

"Please, Stevie."

180

I want to catch another half smile—no, can't then look up to find it's not there—save it for later—that other time—spot on the floor?

"Go on, Sal," Steven offers, "you better—"

"Yes," I say, eyes leaving their spot on the floor, looking up—best keep back the half smile as Steven kept his—just share the other—enough for now—but no, here his is—give mine too then, and a bye or a see you or something—

"Not nice to leave without saying goodbye," Lawrence says stiffly, nails attending to the same clean patch on his robe as he sits down again, "should always say goodbye."

"Bye then."

"I thought you liked being my visitor."

"I did. Very much."

"Did you have a nice time?"

"I did, thank you."

Bespectacled eyes restrict their focus to me. "That's nice," Lawrence concludes for us, inserting a smile, "I had nice time too. And Stevie. So that means we all had a nice time."

"Yes," Steven says, his steps brisk towards the door.

"Thank you for coming," Lawrence says, the smile on his face becoming his own as he catches Steven up to the door, finding ready-made pride in ready-made etiquette. Lawrence reaches past Steven for the handle before the moment's stolen from him—but how can I still be here?—still in the middle of the room in the coat I'd never taken off and the two of them at the open door. I redeem untaken steps with a momentum that carries me back the way I came, already down the stairs and down the street and along the front where it's too late to be remembering to say what you were meant to say—what I meant to say—thank you for having me.

"Sally! Sally! Hey! Stevie's sister!"

Lawrence running after me in his towelling robe and unlaced boots, Steven a way behind, keeping his walk even, his hand up, might be a half smile hiding if I could see.

Lawrence gets his breath back. Not the Lawrence from that first year, not the Lawrence from last night, but this Lawrence, calling after, smiling, smiling, never seen a face so pleased to see my face.

"Yes?"

"You will come back, won't you? You'll be my visitor again."

"Of course," I say, but he's already running back to Steven.

"Thanks for having me!" Meant to say it so I do, shout it after, might have heard me, hope he did.

* * *

Bank holiday wasn't bank holiday without tea at the Grand. But it isn't bank holiday and it isn't time for tea. It is—at least according to the dispassionate pair of chimes whose glum vibration is still caught in the damp air—two o'clock. Two o'clock on the first Saturday of March, though the light-less sky, unconvinced, does little to confirm this—it might have been any unremarkable hour (most likely around five) on any unremarkable day (surely a Monday unless a Tuesday—a Tuesday wouldn't have been altogether implausible) at the end of a year slouching over the next, taking toothless, taste-less mouthfuls out of the months it was too sluggish to make way for. No—no, it is two o'clock, it is Saturday, this is spring.

Over the horizon sandbag clouds bear their weight down on the water, dragging it closer. That hollow sickness in my stomach again, a pinch of acid in the glands. The water was meant to make it better—the sea had always taken the sickness away, only now, looking out, watching the resignation of its indivisible dual task folding back on itself over and over, spittle-specked and grey and green, the sea seems the colour of sickness itself—and seems so heavy—well, whatever it is time for, it is certainly not time for tea—if indeed there is any such thing as tea for one, which I sincerely doubt—unless it came in a styrofoam cup which is what I buy—

"Leave the bag in?"

"Please."

And go and sit on the beach I've no more business sitting on now than I did this morning—except that now—how many were there?, two, three, four, five—five of the Golden Gallopers had found a rider, others waiting, waving, rubbing their hands. I take a spot just a little way up from the carousel and watch the waving and the waiting, sit and watch and drink my tea, sit and watch without waiting or wondering if it would rain—one needless glance up already said it would—or if it would get too cold—I've got my gloves—the gloves—not in my pockets—must have left them at number eight—couldn't go back—not now, we'd said our goodbyes—even had an encore—Steven would pick them up—*Stevie's!*—yes, of course, Steven's gloves—still, could do without having to explain that one to Clive—

"Oh, please can we? Just once! Please!" A triple plea rings out: three girls in matching anoraks and pigtails scampering behind a woman whose arms are full with stuffed winnings, hats, blankets, her head jutting an exasperated stride beyond her step. "Alright, alright!" she says, relenting, a teddy tumbling to the pebbles as one arm tries to contain a load needing two. "Now look!" she says, shaking her purse between the girls and the teddy.

"He's alright, aren't you," one of the girls says, picking the bear up. The other two girls are holding out their hands, ready to have a coin smacked into their palms.

"Last time," the woman says, giving the third her fare, "or we'll be late for tea." She stands for a moment, her back to me, checks the sky, unloads her arms and, after reaching for a strayed hat, unrolls a blanket, lies back, letting the hat fall over her face lest the sky should change its mind. Doesn't seem likely, the sky was set but at least the sickness is going, folding back with the sea's own sickness—yes, it does take it away, always did—just had to keep watching the water, turning back, turning back. The girls' last round would be over any moment—the woman had taken a peek from under her hat and is letting it drop again—scampering back, scampering on, leaving the woman calling after them as she gathers the load.

Carousel's empty now. Walking past, I see the man in its middle slumped, arms cradling his belly, his dropped head serving as a closed sign. Aunt Vivienne used to ask us what we wanted to be when we grew up and for years Steven said the same—that he wanted to be the man in the middle of the carousel. And why, good God, would he want to be that? Because, Steven had explained, then you could go on it anytime you liked … even in the middle of the night.

"Little boys should be asleep in the middle of the night," she'd tell him.

"But I won't be a little boy when I'm the man in the middle of the carousel."

I stop to look back. Wouldn't have been able to tell if it was the same one even if I could see his face—hardly likely—less likely still I'd know the face I'd be looking for—thought I might remember but even if I did it was probably another face I'd found along the way—one with bristled cheeks and tiny black eyes—that seemed to do for the man in the middle of the carousel—at least do for me—the man in the middle of the carousel mightn't be quite so sure. Either way there's enough to contend with trying to keep hold of what is, never mind what isn't—couldn't tell which was which half the time—the man in the middle of the carousel, Lawrence, Steven, the pattern—all just as they were, all going however it went with fish suppers and strolls and paddles—except that it couldn't, maybe never had, and the only pattern is the one still waiting to be made, one where at two o'clock—

"Twenty to, dear."

"Thank you."

Where—at twenty to three even if it does feel more like five, on a Saturday that feels nothing like a Saturday, at the beginning of a spring that feels nothing like spring but is, nevertheless, twenty to three on a Saturday in spring and you find yourself making the beginnings of what might be a pattern—one as good as another—out of rolling up trousers and untying double bows and stepping the feet you'd kept hold of somehow, that you thought you'd never keep hold of but were in the end all you had kept hold of—stepping feet steady enough over the pebbles into the spittle-specked grey-green sickness that takes the sickness away and in ankle-deep for as long as it takes to stop feeling the cold and then having to put socks on wet feet before taking the long way back just to see the fish shop—that was a bead shop where there is no Lawrence but a woman asking if I was after anything in particular—

"No, I was just—"

"Having a browse?"

And knowing you aren't yet ready to go back but not knowing where to go next and still that little part wondering if
Lawrence might appear, that little part listening for Steven's
voice, so hovering about for however long that meant you had
to buy something and so coming away with these packets of
beads—hadn't a clue what to do with them, but still, and then
between there and the guest house rehearsing all the variants
that might explain the missing gloves that weren't even Clive's
to miss only to find no one there and no one who wanted
anything explaining to and that all that was left was to take
those stairs that were just stairs and cross the landing that
was just a—

Yes, Little Miss, just a landing—

After all that, yes—just a landing—and room five just room
five, the same room five and back there now waiting for the
waiting to begin before the dark had even begun to uncover the
light behind the day's lightless sky and with that waiting and
wondering finding all the things that packed and unpacked
themselves were packing themselves up all over again, ready
to leave, waiting for you to pack up the rest, to leave the key on
the table and a note for Clive to say how sorry I was, I'd had to
go but thanks and—

Is that how it would go? Yes, could go something like that—
has to because I've got to go before there's any more waiting
or wondering—only to find, making my way along the front
again, the waiting and the wondering are walking with me,
had packed themselves along with the beat and bows, would
be bringing back all I came with—all that wouldn't be left, all
that made every there the same here—except perhaps, just
before the turning up towards the station, when you were
still on your way—at least this time—and not yet on the train
and there is still far away enough not to be that same here,
when after a day that wouldn't show its light until the sun's

last embers tip the flock of black wings banding into a single gold-flecked black kite flying home to roost on the black bones of the old pier.

* * *

Please remember to take all personal belongings with you.

The bows, the beat—they'd remember themselves. I put my head against the window and wait for the train to empty, the beginning of Saturday nights out fading, the rustle of a bin liner dragged along the aisle. I get up, land in the beer my neighbour spilt three stops ago—he'd looked at the foaming pool between our feet then up at me, edging past carriage etiquette before he peered into his can, trying to get a measure of his loss. He'd pulled down his bag, landing it with a thump into his seat and dug out a towel—an enormous bath towel—urging it towards me, it's alright, I told him—so he just stood there, holding it up like he'd meant to come as a matador but couldn't get the gear together. His face laughed and I felt mine laugh back as he raised his can, "To London," he said.

Why not? "To London," I said, lifting a plastic cup.

He was south of the river, said he hadn't been home in years, left the country enough times but never made it back to London—and it's not like Brighton's far—

You can do it in a day, easy—

Yes, easy, surprised, not for the first time, how simple contact between strangers could be.

"This is me," he said when we got to Blackfriars. "Have a good one and sorry about the …"

I try to picture Steven's face but I can't see it. Come back, I want to say to the blankness pasted over the figure of my brother, just to get me home—but I'm going to have to get home without him—only, waiting for the eighty-two, I know home is not somewhere I'm going—at least not yet. Calling Dad last night had already breached the unspoken pact—we couldn't mention Steven because that would mean admitting what he had left, what we couldn't leave—Dad's Hello for him was all the contract could withstand. I wasn't ready for Dad's sigh, seeing me back two days early, not ready for him seeing but not saying, seeing but not asking—*Are you alright? Is Steven ...* not yet ready to find I still didn't have the answer to the question he wouldn't ask and then watching him absorbed back up that same flight of stairs, the same little chipped white saucer in his hands, up to the infant-mother, her voice tugging me towards her while I sat on the last step, letting my head fall over my bag. I'm not sure where I'm going but it isn't home—

Sweet—

No. The bus passes Platt's Lane without me getting off and a few minutes later I'm walking down Melanie's street. We couldn't have lived much more than a mile apart but it was as though she'd vanished the day her mother came and took away the portraits my grandfather had painted. What am I doing? It's gone eight o'clock on a Saturday night, she might not even be there, someone else will come to the door, see a stranger in me—Melanie and I had known it was one another straight away, but Aunt Vivienne? Uncle Rupert?

"You'll have to come round," Melanie had said, "Mum would love to see you." I'd twitched at that—

Mum would love ... as though it made me disloyal somehow—

What did you say, you didn't tell, what? Tell me—

But my feet, taking me to Melanie's door, couldn't have heard my mother's voice, they had taken their course with a momentum that wouldn't be interrupted; they had a beat of their own.

I don't share their enthusiasm any more than I imagine Aunt Vivienne would share Melanie's. The Aunt Vivienne I see is the one my mother crafted: skin pulled tight over her bones, pencil thin brows and lips, a voice like smoke—a stock type, not a person—the woman who took the last of my grandfather away. The day Aunt Vivienne had taken my grandfather's paintings my mother had taken my face in her hands, pulled it hard towards her and then just dropped it and turned away. She didn't say anything about my eyes or her father's eyes, shut her own and said with a calmness I'd never heard before or since: "Daddy always hated Vivienne."

Could I picture her for myself? Floating a tablecloth down, picking out the white sugar lumps with miniature silver tongs—they had maids, nannies, housekeepers, but Aunt Vivienne, who never took off her apron, insisted on doing certain things herself—removing the bunch of flowers from interfering hands before they became too helpful, sliding the scissors down the cellophane, cutting the stems ... she'd caught me watching her as she arranged them, almost a smile as she took one out and gave it to me—

Could Aunt Vivienne have done that? Yes—she did—and it's only now, twenty years later, right where Dad had dropped Steven and me off and Melanie running towards us, that I remember that the day Aunt Vivienne came and took the paintings away was not the last time I saw her. Steven and I had gone to stay with them, yes—I'd slept on the foldaway in Melanie's room, setting the alarm off because I'd been sleepwalking, our first night Aunt Vivienne letting Claire make us a midnight feast and telling ghost stories until Melanie screamed and Steven put his head between his knees, my shudder caught by the sudden switch of the torch ... two, three, four weeks of breakfasts and bedtimes and school uniforms pressed and folded—was it really as long as that? Why? Try to think when. Before or after my grandfather? After, yes—it was after

189

my grandfather had died, after that night with my mother and the pills—yes, it would have been a few days after that, once Dad had taken her to the place he promised would make her better—the place that never could make her better—Dad had disappeared into the cupboard under the stairs and got out the two smallest cases. Steven had started jumping up the stairs, "We're going on holiday!"

"You're going to stay with Aunt Vivienne. Now, which pyjamas do you want me to pack?"

"But I don't want to stay with Aunt Vivienne," Steven had said, running up two flights and crouching behind the sofa. Dad had to pick him up as he was, head pressed against his knees, and put him in the car. "I'll run away," he said, "I'll run away and find mummy."

I can't remember Uncle Rupert saying much the whole time we were there, but when Dad brought Steven in, still curled up, Uncle Rupert asked Steven if he'd like to help him pick some blackberries. They spent the whole afternoon in the garden and when they came inside Steven stood by the window, quietly saying the names of all the trees and flowers he could remember being taught, like he was practising for a test.

"Who are you talking to?"

"No one."

"Steven's talking to himself."

Uncle Rupert's hand on Melanie's shoulder brought her eyes up and closed her mouth—and a few days later it would be Uncle Rupert who told Aunt Vivienne to keep her voice down about Steven's wet sheets.

But my feet weren't taking me towards Aunt Vivienne, or even to Melanie, certainly not Uncle Rupert who was still, at least in my mind, a gathering of dust, cloud upon cloud up as high as I could see, his low words a diligent ghost train, head always lowered, bending to press his grey lips to Melanie's head, then Claire's, Aunt Vivienne's cheek last. I can't retain a solid enough sense of them, even the house itself, to feel as though that is what I'm just seconds away from—I just see myself in an empty living room, looking up at the eyes in portraits—

Same eyes as Daddy, same eyes as you—

Ayme-eyes-as-daddy-ayme-eyes-a-yoo—

My grandfather's brother's eyes, my grandfather's, mine— Melanie's too. I want to see what I'd been looking through, see if I could see through those eyes back to myself. My own reflection tells me nothing—and maybe the paintings wouldn't either—but my feet are outside Melanie's door—

Perhaps Aunt Vivienne had given me that flower because it was our last day; we'd been waiting for Dad to come and get us but it had been a bit difficult, Aunt Vivienne explained, mummy was still a bit under the weather. Uncle Rupert had dropped us home in the end; he'd kissed the tops of our heads too, the way he had Melanie's and Claire's.

"I suppose you liked staying with Aunt Vivienne, did you?" my mother had asked when we went up to her room. Steven and I had looked down and I'd dropped the hand holding the flower.

"I suppose you'd like her to be your mother, wouldn't you?"

Steven shook his head but I'd looked up, holding the flower towards her, a latent flame flickering in her with my reach, flickering out as I drew the flower back again.

Dad took us to the park that afternoon. Bike rides and ice cream. It could have been any other Sunday. Except if we were

191

going out for bike rides and ice cream it was anything but any other Sunday.

Jewelled hair slides, conspicuous nostrils, the apron she never seemed to take off—I almost mistake the woman at the door for Aunt Vivienne—but I see, after I've finished apologising and explaining myself via Melanie and London Bridge, that it's Claire, flushing in a way that could never have been Aunt Vivienne, her hug tight and breathless as Melanie's.

"We were just in the middle of—", Claire laughs, shakes her head. "I can't believe it's you!" She's already pulling me inside, taking my bag off me. "What are you lugging about with you in this? Moving in?"

"No, I—"

"Mum! Sally's—" she breaks off to turn back round to me, "Mum is going to be thrilled!"

That pang again—

Don't say, you didn't say—

"Now where will we sit you?" Claire looks round the table: Uncle Rupert just raising his eyes from his plate, Aunt Vivienne rising carefully as her smile, mouthing *my niece to* the woman opposite (three unknown mouths *ohhh*, two unknown heads nod), a man I don't recognise holding out his hand, "I'm Claude, I'll get you a chair."

"Thanks, darling," Claire says. "You'll have to make do with us, I'm afraid, Melanie's out on the town for a change. And so this is Martine." A whiskery lady coughs. "This is Victor." A red hand raises a glass above a dropped head. "And last but not least, Sandra—did you ever meet? My partner in crime—"

"I'm sure we must have," Sandra beams. Aunt Vivienne and Uncle Rupert clear their throats.

"And you've met Claude," Claire says just as Claude is coming back in with the promised chair that Claire seems to have understood as sealing our acquaintance. I duck as he lifts the chair high up in front of him, telling Sandra to budge along. Seven pairs of eyes watch me as I sit, six mouths smile—Uncle Rupert permits a nod—Claire's saying she hopes I'm not a vegetarian, Sandra's trying to help Claude remember where he was—

"Stopped and searched—"

"That's right—"

"Oh please don't tell this one," Martine says, hiding her face in her hands as a gleeful Claude goes on.

Uncle Rupert is pouring me wine, his hand on my shoulder—lovely to have you, he says under the medley of laughs for Claude—then for a moment I can't hear anything, I can see all these hands and faces expand and contract, Steven's face almost appears, the infant-mother tugs, my grandfather gasps—

"Now, Sally," Aunt Vivienne's voice slides through, "we want to hear all about you. Sally's my niece, my sister's eldest ..."

I do not know what to say. The heat rising behind my eyes tells me there are tears waiting. I open them wide as though trying to defy them, blink—but they fall and keep falling and the tissue passed along and the silence and Claire's hand on my arm only makes the tears fall hotter and faster—I can't understand how I'm still sitting there but then I realise I can't quite feel myself against my seat, I can't feel my legs to move them—only Claire's hand on my arm and the eyes trying not to look.

Slowly the low voices begin, merge, tentatively gain a little speed and strength. The tears stop, I feel Claire's hand lightly squeeze my arm as she leans to kiss the side of my head.

"Sorry," I say, "ridiculous, I only meant to—"

"Don't be silly, just as well you don't wear make-up—I'd be a fright."

Uncle Rupert catches my eye, touches the bottle. I shake my head.

"Oh yes she will!" Claire tops up my glass. "Now what do you think of my chicken?"

"Claire's a phenomenal cook," Claude says, "the best—except of course for you, Vivienne." Claude looks at me, grins, stage whispers, "Mother's awful."

"Claude!" Martine nudges Victor, "say something."

"Your mother … your …" He reaches for the bottle.

The table has forgotten my tears and I don't think in this moment I have ever felt more grateful. A short memory is the kindest. Mine has always reached too far back—through the infant-mother to faceless faces and doorless houses, to the eyes in the portrait, seeing what they saw, pulling me under. This memory reaches too far to be my own. And yet, somehow I can't even remember the last time I cried before the tears round this table.

* * *

"Stay a bit," Claire says as everyone gets up for coats and goodbyes.

I go into the living room but my grandfather's portraits of his brother aren't there. I scan each of the walls: Melanie's piano certificates, Aunt Vivienne's watercolours …

"Dad's making coffee, do you want?" Claire asks.

"Sure. Claire ..." I check the walls again as though I could have missed them, "... remember the portraits?"

"No, what portraits?"

"Bernard's."

"Grandpa Bernie's?"

"All those paintings he did—of his brother."

"Which ... oh, wait, yes—yes, I do remember, we had them on the floor in the hall for months, mum was going stir crazy about it. We had to cover them with dust sheets I think—you'd think someone had died."

"Where are they now?"

"Vienna I think. Ask mum, I can't remember the story." Claire turned, her mother was coming in. "Mum, Grandpa Bernie's portraits—"

"Vienna, yes, and I was not going stir anything."

"But I thought—" I stop—

Don't say you didn't—

"After your grandfather died his niece—his brother's daughter—she'd been in touch every now and again, trying to find family still alive—your grandfather always said if she came to London she could have the portraits, have something of her father, take his memory of him home. She didn't make it here until after your grandfather's funeral but still ... yes, so they're in Vienna ... I'll go and see what's happening to that coffee ..."

Take the memory of him home. Take something of Bernard back home too.

* * *

At the window there waits the faceless face for the last ghost to take his turn, a turn he has taken and will go on taking until his own face is seen, the face of a man as his ghost wears his face, his face before his face was made a copy, defaced to make a sign, the face of another listed and numbered, another whose number replaced his name, this man, just another, displaced left to wander, a ghost that might find his way home.

ACKNOWLEDGEMENTS

Kate Catchesides, Pele Cox, Rozalind Dineen, Edward Gold, Flora Harragin, Sarah Jones, Kerstin Twachtmann, Trudy White, for all your love and support, thank you.

(And to the incomparable Willow Gold for being Willow Gold.)

ABOUT THE AUTHOR

Miranda Gold is a novelist and playwright. Before turning her focus to fiction, Miranda took the Soho Theatre Course for young writers, where her play, *Lucky Deck*, was selected for development and performance. *Starlings* has also now been adapted for the stage. She is currently based in London.